MICAH McKINNEY
AND THE BOYS OF SUMMER

by Nina Chapman

CAPSTONE EDITIONS
a capstone imprint

Micah McKinney and the Boys of Summer is published by Capstone Editions
1710 Roe Crest Drive
North Mankato, Minnesota 56003
www.capstonepub.com

Library of Congress Cataloging-in-Publication Data is available on the Library of Congress website.

ISBN: 978-1-68446-090-8 (hardcover)
ISBN: 978-1-68446-091-5 (eBook PDF)

Summary: As she starts the summer before middle school, twelve-year-old Micah wants—more than anything—to undergo a miracle transformation. One that will bring with it new friends, a fresh start, and boobs. If that happens, then maybe she can finally forget about what happened in the past. About losing her mom, about losing her best friend, and about the disaster she became in sixth grade, when everything fell apart. But as Micah awkwardly navigates her way through crushes, friendship, and the challenges of becoming a teenager, she discovers that the real transformation that needs to take place is in how she sees herself.

Cover Illustration: Mirelle Ortega

Designer: Hilary Wacholz

Printed and bound in China.
2492

To Walter Gwyn, the best dad a girl could ever have

CHAPTER 1

81 days left

This is how it's going to happen. I'm going to walk into seventh grade with my new friends from my new neighborhood and be a completely different girl. I'll have traded in my old ratty soccer shorts for skinny jeans, and I'll finally have boobs—the round kind.

I opened my eyes and sighed, inhaling the sweet lemonlike scent that wafted over me from the magnolia tree I was hiding under. I felt my body melt further into the grass of my new front yard and closed my eyes again, thinking of all the possibilities. Anything could happen in a new neighborhood. I could be anyone.

It was the second day of summer vacation. That meant I had eighty-one days left. Eighty-one days until the start of seventh grade. Eighty-one days until my thirteenth birthday. Eighty-one days to re-create myself.

Who knew? Maybe eighty-one days would be enough time to forget about what had happened. To forget about the disaster I'd become in sixth grade. Maybe it would be enough time for Libby to forget too. Maybe it would be like nothing had ever happened.

* * *

"Dude . . . is she dead?"

I jerked my eyes open at the sound of a boy's voice, but the Texas sun was bright—too bright. I must have fallen asleep because the shadow of the magnolia tree I'd been hiding under had shifted, leaving me exposed in the grass while three silhouettes hovered above me.

I scrambled to sit up, trying to shield my eyes, and the boy in the middle stepped closer to block the glaring sun. "Better?" he asked.

I froze. He had light-green eyes, smooth, dark skin, and jet-black hair that stood out in tufts . . . but in a cool way, like he'd done it on purpose. Two other boys stood behind him—one was short and scrawny, and the other one was bigger and had a smirk on his face.

The bigger kid peered at me from around the green-eyed boy. "Dude, you've got grass stuck to your cheek. Were you drooling?"

I looked at the first boy again. I couldn't get over his eyes. They were sea green, like the crayon. It suddenly got quiet, and I realized that they were all staring at me staring at him. The mouthy kid snorted, and I blushed, realizing he had said something about drool and grass. I scrambled to my feet and turned my back to them so I could swipe the grass off my cheek in private.

Was I seriously drooling?

"I'm Luke," the green-eyed boy said, interrupting my thoughts. "And this is Ryan." He pointed at the shy kid to his left. "That's Josh." He gestured to the obnoxious one.

"Micah!" my dad shouted, standing next to the moving truck. He was holding a box and struggling to wipe the sweat out of his eye with his sleeve. "Come help me with these last two boxes!"

"I gotta go," I said to the green-eyed boy.

"OK." He smiled a lazy half grin that made my stomach turn a flip. It was like he knew something I didn't. "See ya later, Micah."

"Man, she's lame," the mouthy kid said before turning to walk away. "Let's go to my house."

The other two followed him across the street, both sneaking a second glance as they walked away. They caught me watching them, so I jerked around and headed for the moving truck, where my dad stood waiting for me.

"Well . . . ," Dad said, smiling his teasing grin. "I guess six miles just wasn't far enough."

"What do you mean?"

"We should have moved farther if I wanted to keep the boys away. Probably should have left Wichita Falls. Maybe Texas even."

"Yeah, right," I muttered, snagging the box from his hands.

"I don't know . . . with all these boys flocking over here, I think I'm gonna have to break out the water hose." Dad ruffled my already messed-up hair, making the blond bun on my head bob from side to side.

I ignored him and turned toward our new house. "I'm pretty sure I can just scare them all away with my drool," I mumbled.

"What?"

"Nothing," I said over my shoulder, readjusting my grip on the box. "Where do you want this?"

"Just put it in the living room with the rest. We'll sort them out later."

I paused on the front porch and studied the house in front of me. It was smaller than our old house and nowhere near as pretty. Everything about it was plain and empty, including the porch where I stood. It made me miss our old porch swing and the flowers Mom used to plant under our big oak tree.

My eyes fell back to the massive magnolia tree near the side of the house. I could smell it from where I was standing, and the scent made the knot in my stomach ease up a bit.

As soon as I walked through the front door I felt the cool air gushing from the vents. The power must have finally come on. It smelled weird, like old ladies.

I dropped the box in the middle of the living room floor, and the lid flopped open, revealing our old Halloween decorations. I went to close it, but a small piece of paper poking out beneath a scarecrow arm stopped me. It was an old receipt, just the thing Mom used to draw on. I turned it over, disappointed to find that it was blank.

When Mom was alive, she'd drawn on anything she could get her hands on: receipts, napkins, disposable coffee cups. She always drew the types of things we'd see outside on lazy walks. Things that most people wouldn't notice, like a dandelion squeezing through the cracks in the sidewalk or a feathery seed floating in the summer air.

Later she would leave scraps of her art, little tokens of love, in random places for Dad and me to find throughout the day. I'd discover a drawing tucked inside my lunch box at school or under my pillow at night.

It hadn't stopped in the two years since she'd been gone. I kept finding her drawings all over our old house, hidden in the weirdest places. I'd unearth one tucked inside a shoe or sitting in the pantry on top of the peanut butter.

I had been looking for one of those drawings all day. I needed a sign. I needed to know that she was OK with our move.

I heard Dad walk into the house and felt him slow before he set the box he was holding down next to me. "What are you thinking about, kiddo?"

He had that sad look he would get on his face sometimes. The one he got when Mom came up in discussions. I could tell that he knew I was thinking about her. The same way I knew he was thinking about her too.

"Oh . . ." I stalled. My eyes fell on the box full of costumes sitting in front of me. "I was just thinking . . . that I wanted to be a scarecrow this year. For Halloween, I mean."

It sounded like a lie. Probably because it was.

I quickly started unpacking boxes, hoping he hadn't noticed. It must not have worked because I could still feel him staring at the back of my head.

CHAPTER 2

80 days left

I couldn't shake the gross feeling I got waking up in this weird place. The sunlight was streaming in from the wrong side of the room and into my face. This definitely wasn't home.

I rolled out of bed and trudged past my dad's room, where he lay snoring with his mouth gaping open. The floors creaked as I walked through the empty house toward the living room. I turned on the TV, but found myself staring at a blank blue screen. No service yet. I opened my laptop. No Wi-Fi either.

I sighed and closed the computer again. Dad had said it would probably be a while before the cable guy came, but a girl could hope.

Homesickness started to creep up on me. I had to get

out of there, and I knew just the thing that would make me feel better.

I headed back to my room and threw on a pair of shorts under the T-shirt I had slept in. I didn't even bother readjusting my bun from the day before and tried not to look in the mirror while I brushed my teeth.

After digging around through the boxes in the kitchen for a bit, I finally found a granola bar that had gotten squished under a can of beans. I shrugged. *I guess this will have to do,* I thought. It was that or the leftover pizza from the night before, and to be honest, I was getting pretty sick of pizza.

I pulled my bike from behind another pile of unpacked boxes, threw on my helmet, and jumped on barefoot. I took a bite of the granola bar and sped off, riding as fast as I could go with one hand. As soon as the morning air hit my face, I felt like I could breathe again. I was finally free.

Then it dawned on me. I really *was* free. I could go wherever I wanted in this neighborhood. For once, I didn't have to worry about avoiding certain streets.

In my old neighborhood, if I passed Libby's house, I'd have had to deal with her new friends, Marissa and Samantha, making fun of me for doing "kid stuff." Apparently riding your bike wasn't cool if you were a girl in the sixth grade. I thought that was dumb. I loved my bike.

I rode around, trying to spot houses where kids my

age might live, hoping somebody else around here liked to play outside. I'd been keeping an eye out since we first drove through the neighborhood but hadn't really seen anyone.

Well . . . except for the three boys who'd caught me drooling in the grass the day before. I tried to imagine how I looked with grass stuck to my cheek.

"Were you drooling?" I asked aloud, mimicking the conversation from the day before. "Yeah! I drool all the time." I shook my head and took another bite of my granola bar.

What a weirdo. When did I start talking to myself?

Just then, I hit a huge crack in the sidewalk. I almost biffed it, but gripped my handlebar just in time, losing my granola bar in the process.

"Noooo . . . ," I whimpered.

I glanced back to see if I could spot where I'd dropped it, but the next thing I knew, I was sprawled out on the concrete, up close and personal with a roly-poly that was lazily making its way across the sidewalk. Both of my elbows stung, and I turned my head to see a lone Rollerblade a few inches from my face spinning its wheels at me.

"Did *you* do this?" I asked it.

The wheels just kept spinning, mocking me.

"Are you OK?" a voice shouted from behind me.

I turned to see a pretty girl in a cute yellow tank top and jean shorts hurrying across the yard. Her sparkly sandals gleamed as they flip-flopped in my direction.

I dropped my forehead onto the sidewalk and squeezed my eyes shut. The concrete was warm beneath me, and I wished that I could just melt into it and disappear.

Maybe she'll go away and we can pretend like this didn't just happen.

"Are you OK?" she repeated, rushing closer. "I am so sorry about this!" She knelt beside me. "I told my little brother to pick those up like five minutes ago."

I peeled my forehead off the sidewalk and looked from the Rollerblade to the girl, then back to the Rollerblade. *I hate you,* I wanted to whisper to it. It was bad enough that I had fallen off my bike. It was worse that someone had seen me do it.

The girl tucked her curly, dark hair behind her ear and leaned over me to survey the damage. She grimaced when she saw my elbows. "That looks bad. Come inside, I'll help you get cleaned up."

I got to my feet and kept my eyes down to hide the tears that were pricking up as I followed her down the shrub-lined path to her house. I had a feeling she was close to my age, but she was one of those girls who looked about fifteen. She had curves where I didn't, and actual boobs—like, the for-real kind.

I looked down and realized I was still wearing the shirt with the pizza stain I'd had on yesterday.

Oh . . . well that's cute.

When we got to the porch, the girl turned to me and smiled. "I'm Megan, by the way," she said, holding the door open.

"I'm Micah," I said, trying to smile back.

"Cool name." Megan gestured inside. "Come on in."

The smell of pancakes hit me as soon as we stepped into the house, and my stomach began to grumble. We made our way through the living room, past a couch with perfectly fluffed pillows, until we reached the perfectly white island positioned in the middle of a perfectly clean kitchen.

"Have a seat," Megan said, gesturing to one of the wooden stools lining the countertop. "I'm gonna go see if I can find some Band-Aids to get you cleaned up. I'll be right back."

"OK," I whispered to the now-empty room.

I sat there, looking around at the shiny kitchen. There weren't even any dishes in the sink. My eyes landed on a picture on the refrigerator, and I snuck over for a closer look. It was a cute couple standing on a sandy beach somewhere looking like an ad in a travel magazine. The woman was petite, blond, and fair, and the man next to her looked just as elegant. He was tall and muscular with dark-brown skin and chiseled features.

I stared at the image and wondered if they were actually as happy as they seemed. I thought of the framed pictures that had lined the walls of our old house. Pictures of my parents, eyes gleaming, arms wrapped around each other. They'd seemed happy too, but looks could be deceiving.

"Hey. Micah, right?"

I turned around and took in a sharp breath, choking on my spit, when I realized who it was. The green-eyed boy from the day before stood before me with a crooked grin and no shirt. His hair was messy, like he had just woken up, and he was completely ignoring the fact that I was having a coughing fit. He reached past me, opened the refrigerator door, grabbed the carton of milk, and took a long swig.

Just then, Megan walked back into the kitchen carrying an old first-aid kit. "Luke, have you seen Keaton? He left his Rollerblades out in the middle of the sidewalk again."

"So?" he asked.

"*So*, he made this girl fall off her bike!" She gestured toward me.

Luke looked me up and down, trying to hide the smirk on his face.

Maybe that's why sixth-grade girls don't ride bikes. It's definitely not cool when you fall off.

"I think he went over to play with Josh's brothers," Luke finally said, taking another swig of the milk. "Shouldn't you know that? You're the one who's supposed to be babysitting him."

"No, *we* are supposed to be babysitting him." Megan pulled up a stool so she could fix my wounds—she might as well have been babysitting *me*. "I see you've met my brother." She smiled. "Micah, this is Luke. We're twins."

I took another look at them. I should have realized they were related. They had the same flawless, light-brown skin and sea-green eyes. They even had that same crooked grin, which I'd first seen on Luke when he'd caught me drooling in the grass.

"We met yesterday," Luke said, putting the milk back into the refrigerator and walking out of the kitchen.

"Oh," Megan said. *"You're* the one they were talking about."

Before I could ask what she meant by that, Megan poured peroxide on my arm, sending a stinging sensation down to the bone. The liquid bubbled and dripped down my arm and onto my shorts.

"We might need to do this over the sink," Megan said, leading me around the island.

I flinched when she poured even more peroxide on my arm. This might be it. I was actually going to cry in front of her. I hated crying in front of people.

"So, Micah, what grade are you going into?" Megan asked, trying to distract me.

"Seventh. You?" I tried not to look her in the face. Even her fingers were perfect, with light-pink nail polish that gleamed as she worked.

"We're going into seventh too. Are you going to McNeil?"

I nodded, still gritting my teeth to keep from crying.

"So, Luke says you live down the street from Josh," Megan continued. She rolled her eyes. "Lucky you. He's such a jerk."

I didn't quite know what to say to that, so I just sat there, staring at the pink scar on my knee from the last time I'd fallen off my bike.

Megan finished putting the first-aid supplies back in their box. Then she looked up at me and smiled. "Do you want me to walk you home while I go get my little brother?"

"Sure."

We stood up and made our way out the door toward my bike, which was still lying on the sidewalk. I picked it up, and we walked, side by side, in the direction of my house. I kept hitting my shin on the pedal but ignored it. I wracked my brain, trying to think of something to say, but I came up blank.

"I'm sorry about the Rollerblade thing," Megan finally said, breaking the silence. "Our little brother's six. He's so annoying."

I shrugged. "It's OK. I should have looked at where I was going."

We didn't talk much the rest of the way. A few blocks later, we finally reached my house, and we both awkwardly stood there for a minute.

"Well . . . it was nice to meet you, Micah," Megan said.

"Yeah, you too." I looked down at my bare feet. They looked like boy feet next to Megan's dainty toes.

"I guess I better go get my brother." Megan pointed across the street. "Maybe I'll see you around?"

"Sure." I wanted to say something else, but I couldn't think of anything.

Megan hesitated for a minute, then ran across the street. When she got there, she turned and waved at me again. I waved back and went inside, determined to hide for the remainder of the day.

CHAPTER 3

80 days left

"Where have you been?" Dad asked as I walked in the door. He was sitting at the kitchen table, eating the leftover pizza, and reading something on his computer.

"Just being babysat by a girl my own age," I grumbled.

"What?"

"Nothing, I just rode my bike around."

Dad sat there with his head cocked to the side, looking at my new bandages.

"I fell off my bike."

"Are you OK?"

"Is the Wi-Fi working?" I asked over him, trying to change the subject.

"Not yet, but you won't need it."

"Why not?"

"I got you a membership to the neighborhood pool." Dad slid a card across the table with SEA BLUE printed on it in aqua. "I can only work from home on Wednesdays, so I thought the pool might be a good way for you to entertain yourself while I'm at the office."

I had seen the pool when we'd driven around the day before scoping out the new neighborhood. It was unmistakably old, but still awesome. The high dive looked way taller than the one at my old pool.

I might just have to give up being inside all day after all. But if I did go to the pool, I was definitely *not* going to ride my bike.

* * *

It was ten o'clock, and according to my Sea Blue membership card, the pool was now open. I started sifting through the boxes in my room to find my old green bathing suit. Luckily it was sitting in the bottom of the first box of clothes I dumped onto my bed. I took it into the bathroom so I could see how it fit.

Once there, I shut the door, slipped out of my clothes, and stood in front of the full-length mirror, looking at myself naked. That weird puberty class in school had done nothing to prepare me for what was happening to my body. It was nearly impossible to look in the mirror without freaking out a little. I was kind of getting boobs, but not the cool round ones I saw older girls sporting. And I wasn't as chubby as I'd been a few years ago, but my stomach still pooched out under my belly button.

I looked in the mirror, sucking my stomach in and then puffing it out. I did it over and over again, then wondered if this was normal.

Am I the only person on the planet who does this?

I took one last look in the mirror, surveying the changes. I didn't know if I was turning out normal. How did anyone know that? I knew I had a normal nose because I could see everyone else's nose, but I didn't see everyone else naked. How was I supposed to know that I wasn't a freak?

I couldn't stand it anymore, so I hurried and squeezed into my one-piece bathing suit. It was tight. It was the last bathing suit Mom had bought me, and I'd been wearing it for the past two summers. The straps dug deep into my shoulders at this point, giving the lower half no choice but to ride up. It was like wearing a wedgie magnet.

I turned and studied my backside in the mirror. I definitely needed a new suit, but I was dying to go swimming, so I wore it anyway.

It took me another thirty minutes to find the sunblock, which came out of the tube in oily chunks. I sniffed it, and it didn't smell bad, so I figured it was probably still good. Finally, I pulled on some shorts, grabbed a towel, and headed out the door.

As soon as I stepped out of my air-conditioned house, I started to sweat. It was hot outside, like, *really* hot. I calculated how far I'd have to walk on the hot concrete if I was going to try to look cool. I'd have to go a few blocks to get past Luke and Megan's house and then at least another five blocks after that.

I went ahead and grabbed my bike from the garage. I already looked like a loser in front of the kids in this neighborhood. I had two huge bandages on my elbows, so there was no hiding it.

I'll just make my transformation in high school, I thought as I pedaled off. *I wonder how many days I have until then.*

CHAPTER 4

80 days left

I heard the pool before I saw it. The sounds of kids screaming, whistles blowing, and music playing got louder and louder. When I finally turned the corner, I could see the pool overflowing with people and felt myself start to clam up. Making friends was so much easier said than done. I was tempted to turn back around but forced myself to hop off my bike and walk up to the entrance before I could chicken out.

My bathing suit had now earned its way to thong status, and I was glad that I was wearing shorts. I would have to stay in the water as much as possible to keep people from seeing my constant wedgie. I'd also have to be sure to stay away from the kids with goggles—the little weirdos. You never know what they're looking at down there.

I leaned my bike against the fence next to a bunch of skateboards and walked up to the counter to show my card, but the lifeguards were too busy flirting to notice. The guy lifeguard was snapping his towel at the girl lifeguard; she shrieked and giggled, trying to get away from him.

I felt like a creeper standing there watching them and was thinking about sneaking past when the guy finally saw me. "Oh, hey," he said, sitting down at the counter. "Sorry."

"Yeah, get to work, Andre," the girl teased as she walked out, twirling her whistle on her fingers.

The guy lifeguard—Andre, apparently—pulled his long hair back into a bun, and I eyed the intricate tattoos wrapped around his tan arms.

"You like them?" he asked when he caught me looking.

I nodded.

"They're Polynesian." He smiled.

I didn't know what that was, so I just stood there blinking up at him.

"You must be new," he finally said.

How'd he know?

"The regulars never show their cards." Andre smiled, handing the card back.

Great. I already messed up.

I turned and looked behind me to see a ton of kids my age hanging around the pool in groups. The baby pool seemed like the safest place to put my stuff without being noticed. I made my way in that direction, making sure I was safely hidden behind the moms before I plopped my towel down. Then I quickly pulled my swimsuit out of my butt and took off my shorts. I couldn't wait to jump in the water.

I was heading toward the big pool when I heard someone shout my name. I turned and saw Megan waving me over. She was sitting with two other girls. They were all wearing bikinis and sunbathing on their towels.

"Micah! Come over here!" Megan hollered, motioning to me across the screaming toddlers bobbing around the baby pool.

"OK!" I called back. I tried to smile, but I was pretty sure I looked more constipated than confident.

I went back to get my stuff and headed in her direction. As I walked up, the other girls gave me a look I was very familiar with—like I was disgusting. It was the way Marissa and Samantha had looked at me after Libby decided she didn't want to be my best friend anymore. Libby hadn't looked at me at all.

I put my towel down next to Megan and sat down, which I immediately realized was a big mistake. My bathing suit shifted into a half-wedgie, exposing my right butt cheek. Luckily, I was sitting on it.

"Micah, this is my friend Ava," Megan said, pointing to

a tan redhead wearing a pink bikini that tied at the sides. I didn't even know you could be tan and redheaded at the same time.

"And this is Trish." Megan pointed to the other girl, who had long, light-brown hair and wore lots of eye makeup. I couldn't help but blink every time I looked at her. All the mascara she was wearing was making *my* eyes water.

Goopy eyelash girl gave me a half smile, then turned toward Ava to show her a text message on her phone.

"So, how do your elbows feel?" Megan asked as she lounged gracefully on her towel.

"Oh, they're fine." I wrapped my arms around myself, trying to hide the bandages. It didn't work.

"My mom got so mad at Keaton when she got back from the store and found out what happened. She wants to invite your family over for dinner sometime as a sort of welcome-to-the-neighborhood type thing." Megan rolled her eyes. "She's always doing stuff like that. She said she wants to meet your mom."

"Oh." *What was I going to tell her?*

"Hey, Megan, look at this." Ava interrupted to hand Trish's cell phone to Megan.

Megan looked at the screen and scrunched up her nose as she read the message. It looked like she'd smelled something bad. For a minute I thought it might be me, so I took a stealthy whiff of my armpit as I rested my arms on my knees. I was relieved when all I could smell was the coconut tanning oil the girls were all slathered in.

"He wants to know if she'll be in town on the Fourth to watch the fireworks from the soccer field!" Ava squealed.

"You know what that means!" Trish screamed. She wrapped her arm around Ava's head, covering her mouth with her hand, and pretended to make out with it.

"Ew!" Megan said, handing Trish's phone back to her. "Seriously, Trish, if you kiss my brother I'm going to puke."

My heart skipped a beat.

"But he's so hot!" Ava and Trish said in unison.

Since I was a girl of few words who was currently sitting on an exposed butt cheek, I didn't have much to add. I just sat there and listened to their Fourth of July plans: going to the carnival by the high school and then watching the fireworks on the soccer field. Apparently that was *the* make-out spot for middle school. If you hung out there at night, at least.

As I listened, I wondered if maybe I'd be invited to come along. The thought made me nervous. From the way the girls were talking, they sounded like professionals at kissing. I'd never kissed anyone before, and I wasn't so sure a soccer field was the place I'd want to do it.

Soon the conversation switched to face wash and lip gloss, and I decided I'd had enough. It was scorching hot, and I could feel the sweat trickling down my back. I would have been in the pool first thing if I hadn't been sitting on a problem: I still hadn't figured out how to stand up without mooning the little kids behind me.

While the girls talked, I tried to secretly scoot my butt on my towel, thinking the friction would shift my bathing suit back where it belonged. Unfortunately, it had the opposite effect. I felt the other side slowly shift over, exposing *both* cheeks. Trish looked over at me, and I stopped, realizing I probably looked like a dog scratching his butt on the carpet.

Finally I was so hot and sweaty and tired of listening to girl talk that I decided I would rather show my butt to the whole world than sit there for one more second. I stood up abruptly, fully aware that Megan and her friends had all stopped talking and were looking at me. Ignoring them, I picked my wedgie, walked over to the edge of the pool, and dove in.

My whole body began to relax as soon as I slipped under the water. Everything around me seemed to disappear.

I stayed under as long as I could stand it, hiding from everything that lurked above. I could feel my hair swirling all around me and couldn't help but think of all the times I had played mermaid with Libby. Back when we'd still been friends, when it was still cool to act like a kid. Back when she still liked me.

My lungs began to burn, and I was tempted to flip my hair over my head when I came up for air, just like the little mermaid in the movie. But I thought better of it when I remembered how much water had gone up my nose the last time I'd tried it.

Luckily, I made the right choice coming up like a normal person because as soon as my head broke the surface, I noticed someone watching me. It was Andre, the lifeguard.

I eyed him skeptically. *Can he tell I'm secretly playing mermaid?*

"That's pretty good," he finally said. "How long do you think you can stay under?"

"I don't know." I felt my cheeks go red. "I've never counted."

"Well do it again, and I'll time you."

"OK." I shrugged. I didn't really care if he timed me or not. I just liked what it felt like to be underwater. Down there, I was free to be me. I didn't have to worry about sneering girls with goopy eyelashes.

I went under again, listening to the muffled sounds of people talking overhead and the gurgles of the bubbles as they slipped from my nostrils. When I resurfaced, I realized I had a small audience watching me.

I was rubbing the water out of my eyes when I heard Andre announce, "She did it, boys! She broke the record."

"What?" I heard some boys asking.

"Are you serious?"

Andre nodded. "We've officially got a new kahuna." He looked down and grinned at me.

Ka-what-a?

Some of the boys moaned, and some of them cheered, but the only boy I was looking at was looking right back at me with sea-green eyes and a cocky grin.

"You took my title," he said, staring down at me.

"Sorry. I didn't mean to—"

"No, it's cool." Luke smirked. "I'll just have to beat you and win it back."

"Yeah?" I asked, suddenly irritated. "And what makes you think you could do that?"

I heard Andre laughing from above me.

"Because you're a girl," Luke said, still smiling, "and I can't just sit here and let a girl beat me."

"Aw yeah!" Josh said, bumping his beefy fist against Luke's. "That's what I'm talking about, buddy."

That did it. I glared at him. Sure, Luke was cute and he made my heart flutter, but he was really getting on my nerves.

"Let's do it now," I said. The determination to beat him was bubbling over. I looked at Andre. "Can you time us?"

"Sure." He turned toward Luke. "Good luck, buddy. She's good."

Luke jumped in the water and splashed me in the face.

On the count of three, we both went under. Staying underwater with him there wasn't as comfortable as it had been when I'd been alone. I had a hard time breathing *above* water when Luke was around.

I opened my eyes, feeling the burn of the chlorine as it clouded my vision. I wanted to see if Luke was still there. He was, and I was surprised to find him looking right back at me through the water. I watched as the bubbles slipped out of his nose. I didn't know how much longer I could stay under, but I couldn't let him win.

Finally Luke started to wiggle. A moment later, he broke through the water. I came up right after him.

"Ohhh!" I heard some of the boys taunting. "She beat you!"

Without looking at me, Luke hoisted himself up over the edge of the pool. A kid wearing goggles that pushed his nose up to look like a pig snout pointed his finger in Luke's face. "Ha! Ha! You got beat by a girl!"

"Shut up, Keaton." Luke shoved his little brother into the pool. Then he looked down at me and grinned. "I think you lost something," he said, pointing to the water.

I turned around to see one of the bloody bandages from my elbow floating in front of me.

"Oh sick! It's probably her pad!" Josh laughed.

I grabbed the bandage as fast as I could and started to swim to the shallow end before my face turned red. I tried not to look up at the boys, but I couldn't help it. I glanced up just in time to see Luke turn his head and wink at me.

"We'll see you tomorrow, Micah." He grinned. "Same time, same place." Then he strutted off with his friends while I watched him walk away.

* * *

The lifeguards were flirting again when I passed the hut to leave the pool. The girl was giggling at something Andre had said, and he was holding her hands, trying to pull her closer to him.

I averted my eyes, trying to sneak by without being noticed. I'd almost made it when I heard Andre call out to me. "Hey, wait!"

I turned around.

"Whoa . . . ," he said, staring at my face. "You got some sun."

I touched my cheek. Now that he'd mentioned it, my face did feel a bit tight. Maybe the sunblock I'd put on that morning hadn't been good after all.

"Next time come up to the counter," Andre continued with a smile. "We have extra sunblock up here we can let you use."

"OK, thanks." I turned to walk out again.

"Wait! We forgot to give you your prize."

I stopped. "What prize?"

The girl chimed in, "When someone gets crowned the kahuna they get a free treat from the concession stand. Do you want a nutty buddy or a Popsicle?"

I still didn't know what a kahuna was, but who was I to reject free treats? Besides, my mouth suddenly felt dry. "Can I have a Popsicle?"

"Sure. I'll be right back."

Andre watched the other lifeguard go, then turned to me when she was out of sight. "Don't let them get to you."

"Who?" I asked.

"Those boys."

Ugh . . . he heard them.

"It's not easy getting shown up by a cute girl," he added, grinning at the other lifeguard as she walked back to hand me my Popsicle. "Isn't that right, Charlie?"

She grinned back at him. "I used to kick his butt all the time."

"Still does." He laughed.

"Well, thanks again for the Popsicle," I said, gesturing it toward him.

"Anytime, Micah. Hope to see you around soon. You've gotta keep those boys on their toes." He laughed.

"See you later, Micah," Charlie added, waving as I walked toward my bike.

The Popsicle was melting by the time I got the wrapper off. I was tempted to eat it while I rode home, but then I accidentally bumped an elbow on the chain-link fence reaching for my bike and remembered my crash from that morning. It was probably better if I walked while I ate.

One crash a day is plenty, thank you very much.

CHAPTER 5

80 days left

By the time I got home, my head was pounding and my whole body felt hot, so I took a cool shower. When I got out and looked in the mirror, I knew I was in trouble. There was a perfect outline of where my bathing suit had been, half-wedgie included. The parts that had been covered were sickly white, and the exposed areas were getting redder by the minute.

I gingerly wrapped myself in a towel and sat around for a while, trying to watch TV, but my headache only got worse. I ended up going to bed before my dad even got back from work.

The next morning, I woke up in a cold sweat. My skin felt both cold and hot at the same time, and my eyes felt puffy. I hadn't plugged in the clock on my nightstand yet and had no idea what time it was. I'd fallen asleep naked, and when I tried to put on a T-shirt, it killed my shoulders.

I was in desperate need of water, so I stuck my head out of my bedroom door to see if the coast was clear. "Dad!" I yelled.

It was a Saturday, so he should have been home, but there was no sign of him.

"DAD!" I yelled again, even louder this time, just to double check.

Still no answer.

I had the house to myself—and I *needed* that glass of water. It wouldn't take long to sneak into the kitchen and run back, I decided. There was no need to torture myself by trying to put clothes on.

With one last look around, I dashed out of my room and through the living room, glancing at the clock on my way past. It was nearly noon. I couldn't believe that I had slept so late.

In the kitchen, I threw a Pop-Tart into the toaster and chugged two glasses of water. While I waited for the Pop-Tart to heat up, I looked at my shoulder to survey my skin. It was coated in tiny beads of sweat. I tried to brush them off with my hand, but they burst open, and I soon realized that they were actually blisters.

"Gross," I whispered to myself.

Grimacing, I grabbed my Pop-Tart and started to make my way back to my room. I walked past the mirror hanging in the entryway and stopped abruptly for a double take. I had fallen asleep with my hair wet the day before, and one side was now a mass of crazy waves that went in different directions. The other half was stuck to the side of my sweaty head.

Whoa . . . I look horrible.

Then the doorbell rang.

I froze. I was standing there naked, in front of the door, armed with nothing but a Pop-Tart. I couldn't just run to my room—I'd have to pass a big window, curtains wide open, to get there. I didn't know what to do. I looked to my left and spied the coat closet next to me. Thinking quickly, I flung it open, hoping to find something to cover myself with, but the closet was empty.

Whoever was on the other side of the door started knocking impatiently.

Crap!

I glanced at the floor of the closet and saw a box sitting there. Reaching inside, I ripped out the first thing I laid my hands on—my dad's yellow raincoat. I pulled it on, wincing as the rubbery material touched my sunburn.

"Micah! It's me, open up the door!" It was my dad.

With a sigh of relief, I zipped up the coat and opened the door. The relief immediately vanished when I looked behind Dad and saw Luke, Josh, and Ryan walking up the path.

"Oh, kiddo, your sunburn is worse than I thought." My dad held my chin and surveyed my face, completely unaware of the boys making their way toward the door. "I went to the store to get some aloe vera but forgot the new key." He slipped past me and into the house.

"Nice jacket." I could hear Josh snort. "Why are we here again?" They drew closer to the porch, and I could see Ryan, the quiet guy, staring at me like I was the bearded lady at some freak show.

"Hey, Micah," Luke said, eyeing the rain jacket. "We wanted to see if you wanted a rematch. I've got a reputation to—"

His words jolted me, and I suddenly remembered I was naked under the raincoat. Panic set in.

"I can't!" I screamed, slamming the door in his face.

Without another word, I ran into my room. I flung myself onto my bed and cried. It was so embarrassing. *I* was embarrassing. I wasn't exactly sure why I was crying, but there was no stopping it. I just lay there and bawled until I started to hiccup.

After a while, I heard my dad's timid knock on my bedroom door. "Micah? Are you all right?"

I didn't answer him. I didn't know if I was all right or not.

"Hey, kiddo . . . can I come in?" Dad slowly peered around the door, like he was afraid to take a step farther.

"Yeah," I mumbled, sitting up on my bed. I wiped the snot off my nose with the rubbery material from my sleeve, causing it to squeak.

A smile started to creep onto Dad's face, but I could tell he was trying hard to hide it. "Honey? Why are you wearing a rain jacket?" he asked, easing into the room.

I felt my face crumple again at his question, and a fresh wave of tears flooded my face. I knew I was being ridiculous, but I couldn't help it.

Dad looked startled as he sat on the bed next to me. Between ugly sobs, I told him about my sunburn and how I'd walked through the kitchen naked, only to get caught in the entryway with nothing on hand but a rain jacket and a Pop-Tart.

Dad tried not to laugh as he gave me a hug. I winced when he squeezed my shoulders.

"Sorry . . . here, you might want to put some of this on." With that, he handed me the aloe vera and slipped out of the room.

* * *

Later that night, I was back in my bathing suit—it was the only thing that didn't hurt my sunburn. Dad and I were eating popcorn and watching his favorite movie, *The*

Goonies, for movie night . . . a leftover tradition from when Mom was alive.

"HEY, YOU GUYS!" Dad belted out from behind me on the couch, mimicking the guy with the lopsided face. "Look, Micah! I didn't know you were in this movie."

"Shut up," I said, throwing popcorn in his direction. I turned back to the TV sprawled on my stomach, absent-mindedly swinging my legs from side to side. This of course gave me that stupid lopsided wedgie over and over again. I kept forgetting and had to stop to pull it out from time to time.

"Geez, Micah! You digging for gold there?"

"I can't help it! It's this stupid bathing suit."

When Mom had first bought it for me two years ago, it had been way too big. I hadn't even been able to wear it until the summer after she'd died. Now I got sweaty just trying to squeeze into it.

Dad reached over me and grabbed a handful of popcorn from the bag I was hoarding. He looked at me thoughtfully as he chewed. Finally he said, "Yeah, we're definitely going to have to take you shopping. I don't think you fit in any of your summer clothes anymore."

I sat up. "Shopping? You hate shopping." We both did. Mom had always done it for us. She always seemed to know what I liked, even before I did. That was probably why I'd been putting off asking Dad for a new suit.

Dad pretended to be offended. "Hey, cut me a break. I'm working on it."

"Yeah . . . ," I said, throwing a piece of popcorn in the air, only for it to miss my mouth and hit me in the eye. "Me too."

CHAPTER 6

72 days left

I thought for sure Dad would tell me I couldn't go to the pool for a few days, but all he did was stock up on sunscreen and give me a brief lecture on the dangers of skin cancer. I knew he was right, but I couldn't help being irritated.

If Mom were here, she'd have made sure I put on sunscreen, I thought. Everything would be different if Mom were here.

If she were having one of her good days, she'd have fussed over me and made sure that I was comfortable. It was when I was hurt or sick that I missed her the most. She always knew what to do. Sometimes Dad just seemed clueless.

I holed up in the house anyway, doing what I thought

Mom would tell me to do. Besides, staying inside gave me a good excuse to hide from the neighborhood kids, especially the boys. I seriously had no idea what was wrong with me. Every time I set foot outdoors I did something to embarrass myself. At this point lying low seemed like the best option.

But finally, after a week of self-imposed house arrest, I couldn't take it anymore. My sunburn had gone away fairly quickly, and I figured it was safe to venture out. It was early, and I got so caught up riding my bike in the fresh air that I lost track of where I was going. I ended up peddling past Luke and Megan's house, then past the high school, where I saw the soccer field Trish and Ava had talked about.

Do kids really make out on that field? I wondered. *Will I ever kiss anyone there?*

I rode on and on, letting my mind roam as the warm breeze blew past. Before I knew it, I was looking at the entrance to my old neighborhood. I didn't even know how I'd gotten there. Dad would kill me if he knew how far I'd gone, but that didn't stop me from peddling farther, past the brick entrance to Wellington Estates and toward home—my old home.

When I rode up, I stopped and stared. Angry tears pricked my eyes as I took in the toilet paper strewn all throughout the huge oak tree that took up most of the front yard. I would bet a million dollars that Libby, Marissa, and Samantha had gotten together for one of their sleepovers the night before. Libby and Marissa both lived a few streets over, and for the past year, my house had become the target for their nightly entertainment.

Apparently, they hadn't realized I'd moved. That's how invisible I was.

I wasn't sure how long I stood there, staring at the for-sale sign in my old front yard. It looked out of place, just like everything else. The front porch was bare without the elephant-ear plants my mom had grown every summer, and the grass was tall, which my dad had never allowed when we'd lived there. The whole house seemed lonely and neglected, like a dog that had been left behind to fend for itself.

I looked at the garage and swallowed hard, remembering what had happened there. Then I looked at the tree filled with toilet paper, and suddenly all I could see was the way it had looked that night with the red and blue lights flickering through its bare branches.

My eyes darted over to the garage and back at the tree, no longer flashing red and blue but draped in white. Angry tears spilled over as I tore down all the paper I could reach. I bunched up as much as I could fit under my arm and peddled in the direction of Libby's house, not even caring if she and her friends were outside to make fun of me.

I turned onto the street a few blocks over, and from a distance, I could see the familiar white Jeep parked in Libby's driveway. I knew that house like the back of my hand. I'd probably spent nearly as many nights there as I had in my own home.

Libby and I had been friends since the first day of kindergarten, when I pushed Talon Spencer for squishing a ladybug that Libby was playing with and making her cry. After that it was a done deal. We were best friends.

Libby's mom, Kristen, ended up becoming friends with my mom too, and after Libby's parents divorced, we saw even more of them. Mom invited them over all the time, especially after soccer games, since Kristen coached. Eventually they started to feel like an extension of the family. Sometimes, if our moms drank too much wine during dinner, we'd have a big slumber party where both Libby and Kristen would spend the night. Libby and I would be snuggled up in my room, sharing secrets and giggling, while Kristen and my mom sat on the porch swing, sharing secrets and giggling too.

It was perfect . . . until it wasn't.

Old memories overwhelmed me, and I peddled even faster, clutching the wad of toilet paper until I was in front of Libby's house. The sprinklers were going, but it didn't look like anyone was home.

Struck with a brilliant idea, I thrust the load of toilet

paper I was carrying into the spray and made the biggest spit-wad-looking thing I had ever seen. Then I stared up at Libby's bedroom window on the second floor, gritted my teeth, and hurled the spit-wad at it as hard as I could. It stuck with a satisfying splat. Satisfied, I wiped my hands on my T-shirt and hopped back on my bike, and headed back to my new house.

CHAPTER 7

72 days left

Before long, I was back in front of the high school again. There were people playing on the soccer field now, and for a moment I was tempted to cross the street and ride in the opposite direction, but the desire to get home quickly beat the desire to avoid people, so I stayed on course. It wasn't until I got closer to the field that I realized the players looked all-too familiar.

"Hey, Micah!" a voice called out. It was Josh, holding his water bottle and leaning against the fence. "Where's your rain jacket?"

The other boys were still playing on the field, but once they heard him call my name, they all stopped and started to jog toward him. I could feel my face getting hot as

44

I peddled closer. Whether it was from my leftover sunburn or embarrassment, I wasn't sure.

"Look! She's blushing—"

"Shut up, Josh." I recognized Luke's voice in the jumble of boys.

"Watch this." Josh looked around to make sure he had an audience.

"Don't, dude," I heard someone say.

"Hey, Micah!" Josh called. "We need another player. Why don't you come play?" Some of the boys behind him snickered.

"Dude, leave her alone," Luke said. I felt my heart flutter. "There's no way she could keep up." It immediately sank.

"I know," Josh said. "It'll be funny."

I'd had enough. Before I even had time to think about it, I turned my bike in the direction of the chain-link fence that surrounded the fields and rode toward him.

"Thatta girl, Micah." Josh hooked his fingers through the fence. "Show us what you've got."

I climbed off my bike and stood at the fence, glaring at the boys on the other side.

"She's just going to slow us down," Luke said under his breath. Then, turning to me, he gave a pitying look. "Don't worry about it, Micah. You don't have to play."

My heart pounded in my ears. Not because I liked him,

but because I wanted to beat the crap out of him—out of all of them.

A part of me was tempted to get back on my bike, but before I could give it a second thought, I leaped over the fence, glad I didn't land on my face.

"All right!" said Josh with a glint in his eye. "She's come to play with the big boys! What do you want to be, shirts or skins?"

"Shut up, Josh!" Ryan piped up.

I was surprised. I'd never heard him say more than one word.

"What? Look at her." Josh pointed at me. "She's got nothing to worry about. It shouldn't matter."

"Yeah, but you do," I sneered at him. "Where's *your* bra?"

"Dude!" One of the boys laughed and bounced the soccer ball off his head. "You just got owned!"

The other guys were bent over in laughter, and one of them snuck up behind Josh, grabbed his chest, and gave it a quick jiggle.

Josh's face turned red. "Knock it off!" He looked like he was going to charge at me, but Luke grabbed me by the arm and led me away.

"You can be on my team," Luke said, trying to stifle his laughter. "We need someone at left middle." He paused, then looked at me doubtfully. "You do know what that is, don't you?"

"Yeah, I know what it is." I glared at him, feeling the anger build up in the pit of my stomach. Without giving him a second glance, I got into position.

Ryan tapped the ball to Luke, who launched it into play. The game was fast-paced, but the boys were determined to keep me out. At one point the ball was lobbed in my direction, and a tall gangly kid—who was supposed to be on my team—pushed me out of the way to head it. It bounced off his ear and ended up going out-of-bounds.

I glared at him. *You're an idiot,* I said with my eyeballs.

It became very clear that if I wanted to get any action in this game, I would need to take it. Finally, another kid got a breakaway on my side of the field. He juked past the annoying tall guy and headed my direction.

I stood between him and the goal. The boy tried to fake left but went right. I waited until he was right next to me, and we were running side by side toward the goal. Then I slid just in time to steal the ball out from under him.

The boy toppled over, and I popped up with the ball still in my possession. I took off down the field, my heartbeat echoing in my ears as I dribbled up the field.

"Right here!" Luke yelled as he ran up the center of the field alongside me.

I was nearing Josh, who was playing sweeper on the other team. He came at me like a wild boar, but I passed to Luke just in time and ran around him, heading straight for the goal. Luke lobbed the ball back to me, and I took the shot. It landed in the net with a satisfying whooshing sound.

"Yeah!" I could hear Luke cheer.

Bam! Suddenly something plowed into me from behind. The next thing I knew, I was sprawled out on the ground with a mouthful of dried grass.

"What the heck, Josh? You can't just hit her from behind like that!" Ryan shouted. "She already scored!" He bent over me and gingerly took hold of my arm to help me up. "Are you OK?" He was looking at my face, and I could see the pity in his dark-brown eyes.

I could taste blood, and it felt like I had scraped the left side of my face. I touched it and winced. My cheek didn't seem to be bleeding too badly, but I had a fat lip.

Some of the other guys came closer to get a look, and the expressions on their faces told me it wasn't too pretty. Nobody said anything, but I couldn't take them staring at me any longer. I could tell that they felt sorry for me. I hated that.

"Are we going to play or what?" I demanded, clambering to my feet. Without another word, I jogged back to my position.

"You should have passed it," the tall kid mumbled as I ran past him. I glared at him until he looked away.

"You heard her, get into position," Luke ordered.

Everyone got back into place, and for the rest of the game, the ball was passed to me, and the annoying kid stayed out of my way. My lip jiggled every time I ran. After about an hour we stopped for a water break, but it didn't matter because I didn't have any.

"Here, you can have a drink of mine," Luke said, handing me his water bottle.

"Oh . . . check it." Josh elbowed Luke in the ribs.

I turned to see what had caught their attention and saw Megan, Ava, and Trish making their way across the pitch. All three girls wore matching short shorts and coordinating tank tops in different colors.

"Damn, your sister is hot," Josh said.

Luke punched his shoulder. "Shut up!"

Trish sauntered up to the boys and rested her elbow on Luke's shoulder, artfully twisting a blue lollipop in her mouth. "Whatcha doing?" She grinned.

Seriously? I tried not to roll my eyes but grinned back when I noticed that her teeth were tinted blue.

"What does it look like they're doing?" Megan asked, pointing to the field. Trish pouted at her.

"Why don't you guys ever ask us to play?" asked Ava.

Luke smirked. "Because you'll slow us down."

"Then why is *she* here?" Trish piped up, giving me the I-just-smelled-something-really-bad look she seemed to have glued to her face when I was around.

"Because she's different." It was Ryan. His eyes dropped as soon as they met mine.

"I'll say," Trish mumbled.

Josh laughed.

"Don't be stupid." Megan glared at her brother. "We're just as good as you are! We play club ball too, you know!"

"We don't have time to play fluff ball with a bunch of girls," Luke said. "We're trying to make varsity at Rider when we get to high school."

"First," Megan said with a sassy wave of her finger, "high school is, like, two years away. Second, freshmen never make varsity—"

"We'll see about that," Luke interrupted, wearing his cocky grin.

"And third, we'd like to make varsity too!" Megan finished indignantly. "But that's kind of hard to do when y'all are always hogging the field." Then her eyes focused on me with a quizzical look. "Seriously, though. Why *does* Micah get to play?" She sounded genuinely curious.

"Because Josh couldn't keep his mouth shut," Luke said, grinning. "And then Micah ended up kicking his butt." He winked at me, grabbed his water bottle from my hand, and took a long drink.

Trish and Ava stared at me in shock.

"What happened to your lip?" Megan asked me.

"She couldn't handle the big boys." Josh smirked, looking around for approval from the other guys. Nobody laughed, and Megan looked at him as if he were the foulest thing on the planet. His embarrassment was etched on his face.

I didn't know why, but in that moment, I felt kind of bad for him.

"Are you on a team?" Megan asked me.

"No."

"Where did you learn to play?"

I hesitated for a bit. "I used to play, but I quit."

"What team did you play for?"

"The Strikers," I said, kicking the ground.

"Really? They were our biggest rival when we played rec, but I don't remember you."

"Yeah. Well, I quit like a year ago."

"Oh. My. Gawd." It was Trish, breaking up each word to make sure that everyone was paying attention to her. "I remember you. You used to be fat, didn't you?"

"Trish!"

I could feel Megan's pity without even looking at her. Instead, I trained my eyes on a red ant making its way across the dirt and stepped on it.

"You were their sweeper, weren't you?" Trish continued. "You were like a bulldozer."

Ava suddenly decided to join in. "I remember her!"

"Me too," said Megan. "You were good."

"Not *that* good." Trish huffed.

"Why did you quit?" Megan asked.

I shrugged, hoping she would just drop it. The truth was, I hadn't really wanted to quit. But after everything that went down with Libby and her new friends, it had seemed like the only thing to do.

"Are you looking for a new team?" Megan asked.

"What?" I asked, not paying attention.

"Do you want to be on a team? One of our best players is moving to Oklahoma City, and we're looking to replace her."

Trish looked at Megan with wild eyes, letting her—and everyone else—know that she thought it was a stupid idea.

"I don't think so," I replied. "I don't really play soccer anymore."

"You could have fooled us," Luke said.

Ryan gave me a shy smile. "You should do it."

"Why wouldn't you?" Luke pressed. "You're already better than most of the girls on that team."

Trish and Ava exchanged glances, and Megan glared at her brother. "Thanks a lot."

"It's true," Ryan muttered.

"Yeah, but she's not a hottie." Josh leered as he squeezed his way between Megan and Trish, putting his arms around their shoulders and facing me.

Megan shrugged his arm off her shoulder. "What are you talking about?"

"All the girls on that team are hot, and let's face it," he said, turning to me. "You're not."

"Why do you hang out with him?" Megan asked, looking at her brother. Then she turned to me and said, "Don't listen to him. We play for the same club team as the boys. It's called Xpress."

I remembered the team and their expensive bags and gear, but I didn't remember any of the players. I guess I'd had other things on my mind at the time.

"Anyway," Megan persisted, "tryouts are in August. You should seriously think about it."

I didn't say anything, hoping she would let it go. As much as I appreciated the invite, there was no way I was going to play soccer again. Those days were over.

CHAPTER 8

69 days left

It had been a few days since Megan's invitation to try out for soccer, and I hadn't dared breathe a word about it. I was afraid that if I brought it up, Dad would go back to asking questions about what had happened with my old team—why I'd quit in the first place.

So when he came home from work to find me hugging a bag of chips and watching soccer on TV, I didn't say a word. Without taking his eyes off the screen, Dad joined me on the couch, then reached over, snagged the bag out of my lap, and dug in.

I sat there silently, thinking about my old soccer gear, which probably didn't fit anymore. I couldn't even try out if I wanted to. Then I wondered where my soccer ball was. It probably wasn't the right size either. I vaguely remembered

Libby's mom telling the team we'd size up as soon as we moved age brackets.

On TV, the player rotated the ball over and over in his hands in preparation for the shoot-out. It didn't look much larger than the ball the boys and I had played with the other day.

"I wonder how big their balls are," I said, thinking out loud.

Dad looked at me, and I instantly cringed. *Whoa. . . . That didn't come out right.*

I cleared my throat. "I mean . . . I wonder what size balls they have." *Ew! That didn't come out any better!* "I mean . . ."

My dad snorted in his chips. "Micah, I think you should stop while you're ahead."

My face turned red. I couldn't believe I'd just tried to talk about balls with my dad. I wished Mom were here to buffer the awkward. I didn't remember things ever being this complicated before.

In that moment, the player scored the winning goal.

Dad crumpled up the empty chip bag and turned to face me. "Do you miss it?" he asked.

I played dumb. "Miss what?"

"Soccer, silly. I still don't get why you quit. You were so good."

I looked down and shrugged, pretending to be really interested in the hole in my shirt.

"It was really good for you too," he continued. "It seemed like it helped take your mind off everything."

Yeah . . . until it didn't. I could feel the old bitter feelings start to fester again. He had no idea that he was part of the problem. If I played things right, he'd never know.

I sat up taller, getting ready to bolt. I could tell Dad sensed it because he changed the subject. "Why are you wearing that holey old shirt?"

I shrugged. "It's comfortable."

Dad ran his fingers through his hair, suddenly seeming sad. "I promised to take you shopping, didn't I?" He looked at me kind of sheepishly. "I'm sorry I've been putting it off. I'm not very good at this stuff. Not like your mom was anyway."

And just like that, my anger vanished. He missed Mom as much as I did.

"It's OK. I don't like shopping either."

Dad sat up on the edge of the couch. "Well, I think it's time. Get cleaned up. We're going shopping."

"What? Like . . . now?"

"What else are we going to do? The game is over. Come on. Let's get going before I change my mind. We'll pick up some dinner on the way back."

* * *

The next thing I knew, I was standing in the bathing suit section at Target, feeling like an imposter. I had outgrown the kids' section and was looking around without a clue. Once Dad saw all the bikinis he mumbled something about having to look for a new water hose and left me to fend for myself.

I flipped through the racks filled with different kinds of swimsuits, not really knowing what I was looking for. Quickly, I grabbed three suits and bolted for the dressing room.

I tried on the one-piece first. As soon as I had it on and looked in the mirror I couldn't help but laugh. It was a black suit with big blue flowers printed all over it and looked ridiculous on me. The boobs were too saggy and so was the butt. It was definitely meant for a grandma.

The next suit I tried on was a light-blue bikini that tied at the sides, like the one Ava had been wearing at the pool. It was really pretty, but it made me feel uncomfortable as soon as I looked in the mirror. I looked too . . . grown-up in it. I pulled the bikini off quickly, knowing that I would never be able to wear that in public and not feel weird.

I had saved the tankini for last. I put it on with my back facing the mirror and gasped when I turned around and saw myself. It didn't even look like me staring back. It was bright red with metallic stripes, and it made my skin glow, even in the drab florescent light of the dressing room. A string tied around my neck, and another tied around my exposed back, but the front draped down to cover my stomach.

I was surprised at how long my legs looked and how the top clung to my chest. It proved that I wasn't such a little kid anymore. I loved it so much that I did a little silent dance in the dressing room . . . until I tripped on my shoes on the floor and banged one of my hurt elbows on the wall.

I quickly straightened up, trying not to laugh as I put my clothes back on. Then I headed out to see what other clothes I could find. This shopping business wasn't so bad after all.

CHAPTER 9

68 days left

The next morning, I pulled on one of my new outfits—a pair of jean shorts and a white top—and studied myself in the mirror. I looked like the kind of girl I wanted to be—the kind of girl who could make friends and keep them—but I felt weird. I kept pulling the top away from my body, trying to stretch it out a little. It was tighter than the shirts I was used to wearing. Eventually I quit tugging and undid my braid, letting my hair trickle down my back.

I was still inspecting myself in the mirror when the doorbell rang. I assumed Dad would get it since he was working from home, but the bell rang again, so I went to go see who it was. When I opened the door, I was surprised to find Luke standing there holding a basket full of vegetables.

"She lives!" he said. He stood there awkwardly for a moment, just looking at me, then cleared his throat. "I've been waiting for you to come back to the pool, so I can win my title back. But you never show up."

I felt the blood rushing to my face as he looked at me. I pointed to the vegetables in his basket to shift his attention. "So you thought you'd bribe me with vegetables?"

It was the first time I had seen Luke flustered. "Uh . . . actually, my mom sent them over. They're from our garden. It's mostly zucchini."

"Thanks." I waited for him to hand me the basket, but he kept holding it.

"There's also an invitation to have dinner at our house sometime. Is your mom here?" He looked down at his shoes, clearly embarrassed. "My mom wanted me to make sure your mom got the invitation. So . . . is she here?"

I hesitated for a minute. I hated when this happened, the first time I had to tell someone. I figured it was like ripping off a Band-Aid—the sooner I got it over with, the better.

"She's dead," I blurted out.

Luke's head jerked up, and he blinked a few times. "What?"

"My mom. She died a few years ago. When I was in fourth grade."

"Oh." Luke's face flushed for the second time. "How?"

I didn't know what to say to that question. I never knew

what to say. "Carbon monoxide." It was the same explanation my dad had given me.

"Oh."

He was confused, and I was relieved. That meant he wasn't going to ask any more questions.

"My dad is here, though," I finally offered. "Do you want to come in?"

"Um, sure." Luke finally handed me the basket and stepped inside.

I led him into the kitchen, where my dad was drinking coffee and reading the news. "Dad, this is Luke," I said, setting the basket on the kitchen counter.

"Oh." He eyed Luke up and down. "It's nice to meet you, Luke. I'm Brent, Micah's dad."

I rolled my eyes. "Dad, he knows you're my dad."

"It's nice to meet you." Luke held his hand out for a handshake. I had never seen a kid do that before. My dad looked just as surprised but took his hand anyway.

Luke grimaced a bit at my dad's grip and shook it out when he thought no one was looking. Then he said, "My mom wanted to invite you guys over for dinner. She feels bad for when Micah crashed in front of our house."

My dad shot me a confused look. I pointed to my elbow with the scab still clinging to it.

"Oh, she didn't have to worry about that. Micah crashes all the time."

"Dad!"

"Well, not all the time. . . ." Dad cleared his throat. "Would you like something to drink, Luke?"

"No thanks, I'm going swimming with some friends," Luke replied. "The pool opens in just a few minutes." He looked at me. "Do you want to come?"

"No, that's OK."

"Come on. You can't steal someone's title and then just disappear. You've gotta give me a chance to win it back."

Dad looked from Luke to me and back again with an expression that clearly said he had no idea what we were talking about.

"She beat my record for staying underwater the longest," Luke clarified. "Now she's the kahuna, and I want my title back."

My dad looked at me, impressed. "Kahuna, huh?"

I blushed. "Yeah, I guess." *Whatever a kahuna is.*

Luke glanced at his phone. "Oh man, I gotta go. Meet me at my house in ten minutes, OK?" He started to offer his hand to Dad for another handshake but thought better of it and waved instead. "It was nice to meet you Mr. . . ."

"McKinney. But you can call me Brent."

"OK, Brent." Luke headed for the door but stopped and turned just before he let himself out and pointed straight at me. "My house. Ten minutes. I have a reputation to protect."

I could feel Dad's eyes boring into the side of my head as I pretended to be really interested in the zucchini sitting in front of me, but Dad kept staring. Finally I looked up.

"The water hose . . . ," he said. "I'm going to have to break it out."

"Whatever!" I said as my face grew red. "His mom made him do it."

"Do you want to go over there for dinner sometime?"

I shrugged. "Sure. Do you?"

"Do you think she's a good cook?"

"Probably. Their whole family is perfect."

"Let's hope not," Dad said, patting me on the back. "That'd sure be boring."

CHAPTER 10

68 days left

Ten minutes later, I was standing on Luke and Megan's front porch, about to ring the doorbell, when I heard someone walking up behind me. I was wearing my new bathing suit, and my blond hair was tickling my exposed back.

"Who's *that*?"

I knew that voice. It was Josh. I turned around just in time to see him and Ryan walking up the path.

"Oh, it's you," Josh said. "What are you doing here?" Before I could answer, he reached for the door and let himself in.

Ryan brushed passed me, following Josh into the house. "Hey, Micah."

"Hey," I half whispered. I stood at the front door, not

knowing whether I should follow the boys in or not. Luckily, a short, blond woman with the same sea-green eyes as Luke and Megan appeared in the doorway before I had to decide.

"Hello! You must be Micah," she said, stepping aside. She motioned for me to come in. "I'm Sandi. Luke said you'd be coming by."

I smiled back at her. "Hi," I said shyly. I followed her to the kitchen, where the guys were already helping themselves to whatever was in the refrigerator.

"Here, Micah, catch!"

I looked up just in time to see a can of soda hurtling toward me. I squealed as the cold aluminum smacked my chest, but I couldn't catch it before it fell to the floor. All three boys stood there laughing at me as I bent down to pick it up.

"Luke!" Sandi scolded.

"Just leave that one on the counter." Luke ignored his mom and grabbed another one. "Do you think you can actually catch this one?"

"Sure, if you give me some warning!"

He tossed me another one, then headed toward the hall to what I assumed was his room and disappeared through the doorway. Josh and Ryan followed, but I stayed put.

Luke poked his head out the door. "You coming?"

"Uh, yeah," I said, following in their direction.

Luke's room was the only messy place in the entire house, but it still smelled like clean laundry. The gray walls were covered in framed posters of every sport, and the bookshelves were lined with trophies.

Josh lay down on the unmade bed, propping his dirty shoes on Luke's pillow, pretending to read a comic book. Ryan sat at Luke's desk, browsing for skateboard fails on YouTube. Luke was digging in his closet as I hovered in the doorway. Before I knew it, Megan was standing next to me, poking her head into the room.

"Hey, Micah," she said. "What are y'all doing?"

"We're getting ready to go to the pool," Luke said, pulling out an old yellow skateboard from his closet.

"Oh."

"You wanna come?" Josh asked us, still lounging on Luke's bed.

Megan just ignored him and looked at me instead. "Ava and Trish are on their way over. You want to hang out with us?"

"No way," Luke said. "We've got some business to attend to." He handed me the skateboard. "Do you ride?"

I held up the board. "You mean this?"

He just looked at me like I was stupid.

"No. Not really," I mumbled.

"Didn't think so. You can have this one to practice on. I have a longboard."

"I thought we were going swimming," I said, confused.

"How do you think we're going to get there?"

"She's totally going to bust her face," sneered Josh. He was pretending to read the comic book again, but it was upside down. "Oh wait. She already did."

"Looks fine to me," Ryan piped up from the laptop. "I mean—it doesn't look busted up anymore."

"We're doing makeovers." Megan looked intently at my face. "You should stay with us. Your eyelashes would look amazing with some mascara. I had no idea they were so long. They're so blond."

"Nope," said Luke, wrapping his fingers around my arm and dragging me out of his room. "Like I said, we have business to attend to." He gave me that crooked grin again before letting go. "I've got to win my title back."

"You were serious about that?" Megan asked, rolling her eyes as she followed us back into the kitchen. Josh and Ryan followed us as well. "She beat you. Let it go. Besides, aren't you a little old to be worried about that stupid pool game? I mean, how dorky can you get?"

"First of all," Luke said, turning to face her, "being the kahuna is *not* kid stuff. If you're the kahuna you're basically the biggest, baddest dude at the pool. Just ask Andre. And second, Micah didn't beat me. She just got lucky, is all." He opened the fridge and turned to me. "Hey, Micah, hand me that soda? I can probably put it away now."

I went to grab it, fully aware that my arm was still tingly from where his fingers had clinched it moments earlier.

"Who got lucky?" I heard a girl's voice ask from behind me.

I turned and saw Trish walk into the kitchen, followed by Ava, who was looking down at her phone. Trish's smiled dropped as soon as she turned away from Luke and was facing me. She grabbed the soda out of my hand and started to pull open the tab.

"I wouldn't—" I started to say.

"You can share," she said, in a sickly sweet voice as she turned away from me and popped it open. The soda immediately spewed into her face, making her bangs flop into the air. When she whipped around to face me, I could see her mascara running down her face.

"Whelp . . . gotta go!" Luke grabbed my arm once more and tugged me toward the garage door. He stopped in the doorway and turned to face the girls. "Clean this up," he added, twirling his finger in the air to indicate the mess. He laughed and bolted out the door, dragging me with him.

Josh and Ryan ran after us, slamming the door behind them as we heard Trish scream.

"That. Was. Classic," Josh said as he hunched over laughing. He hopped on his skateboard and glided down the driveway to the sidewalk, chuckling to himself. "Classic."

Luke and Ryan went to get on their skateboards too but stopped and looked at me when I didn't follow them.

"I left your skateboard in the kitchen," I said, glancing over my shoulder.

"You do *not* want to go back in there." Luke laughed. "Trust me."

Ryan skated back toward me. "Here, get on mine."

"That's OK. I don't know how to ride anyway. I can just walk."

"I'll teach you," he offered, holding out his hand for me to balance while I stepped onto his longboard.

"Yeah, we'll teach you," Luke said, holding his hand out on the other side.

Josh shook his head. "You've got to be kidding me." But he stepped off his skateboard anyway.

I stood on the skateboard and held my arms out for them to grab on to. Luke and Ryan walked on either side, dragging me along with them. I rode nearly all the way to the pool like that until we reached the last hill.

"She's never going to learn how to ride like that," Josh said when we paused at the top. Without warning, he placed his hands on both sides of my waist and shoved me from behind. I wobbled and nearly fell off, but before I knew it I was plummeting down the hill.

I let out a shriek and lurched forward once more, nearly toppling off, but managed to regain my balance. Soon my scream turned into laughter, and a grin spread across my face as the warm air whipped through my hair. I was just about to celebrate my victory when I noticed that the street turned at the end of the hill.

"What do I do?" I screamed. I had no idea how to turn. I barely knew how to balance, but I was too far away for the boys to hear, let alone help.

I didn't have time to think. Before I knew it, the skateboard hit the curb, and I was hurtling toward a kiddie pool sitting in the middle of a lawn. The next thing I knew, I was sitting upright in the middle of the pool, facing away from the street. I just sat there in stunned silence while water dripped off my nose.

I heard the boys yelling behind me and turned to see them sprinting down the hill, jumping and pumping their fists in the air. "Yeah! That was awesome!" they screamed.

There was nothing left to do but throw my fist into the air too from where I sat in the middle of the kiddie pool.

"Holy crap, that was the sickest thing I've ever seen!" Josh shouted, pushing me back into the pool while I struggled to get out.

I looked around and realized that this place was kind of creepy. There were no little kids in sight, but dismembered toys lay everywhere.

Ew! I thought as I slipped on a decapitated doll. *Where's its head?*

Luke and Ryan grabbed me by my hands and hoisted me up just as the lady who owned the house opened her front door and started shouting at us. "Excuse me!"

"Run!" yelled Josh, pushing me out of his way.

"Where's my skateboard?" asked Ryan.

"Who cares? We'll come back later!"

CHAPTER 11

68 days left

I followed the boys to the pool entrance, past Charlie, who was working the counter. "There she is!" she said, watching us all walk in. "I was wondering when the kahuna would return."

"Yeah, we'll see about that," Luke said, giving me a playful shove.

We went straight to the pool, where some of the other guys we'd played soccer with earlier in the week were already waiting. Andre was on lifeguard duty, towering over us from his chair.

"Ah . . . the kahuna returns," he said, smiling down at me.

"About time," Luke grumbled. "Now we've got to set

things straight so I can win my title back. Andre, can you time us?"

"Sure you want to do that?" Andre asked. "I mean . . . she beat you pretty bad last time."

Luke scowled. "No, she didn't."

I left them arguing while I went to find a place to put my towel. I ended up setting it down in a pile by the boys' stuff, then heading to the edge of the pool. Soon the rest of the boys gathered around Luke to watch.

"Come on, Luke," Josh encouraged. "You can't let her beat you this time."

I ignored him and jumped into the pool. Luke followed shortly after, and we both waited for the signal. As soon as Andre said, "Go!" we sank underwater.

I made sure to close my eyes this time. It was easier that way, but even with my eyes closed I could feel Luke's presence. I tried my best to ignore it.

I stayed underwater for what felt like forever, enjoying the silence and the way my hair swirled around me and tickled my shoulders. Before I knew it, Luke was shooting up for air.

I waited a moment longer before I resurfaced too.

Andre shook his head. "Sorry, man. She's still got you beat. In fact, she just beat her old record by two seconds."

"Seriously?" Luke slapped the water. "What are you, part fish?"

I smiled and shrugged. *Mermaid, actually.*

Luke demanded another rematch, and every time we went under, I got better at ignoring the fact that he was underwater with me. I felt less nervous around him and instead I just enjoyed the way it felt to float in weightless silence. Luke, on the other hand, got more and more agitated every time we came up.

On the final round, I slid under and used my arms to help me stay seated at the bottom of the pool. I liked how fluid my limbs felt beneath the water, like I was performing a silent dance. Eventually my lungs started to burn again, and before I came up, I opened my eyes to see Luke watching me again.

There was something about the look on his face, like he saw me in a different way underwater. It made me wish I really were a mermaid. If I were, I would swim up to him and give him the air hidden in my lungs, so he could stay under the water with me forever. I locked eyes with him, imagining what it would feel like to touch my lips to his, when Luke broke the surface once again.

"Come on!" he gasped, clinging to the side of the pool. "One more time."

"Sorry, man," Andre said, "I can't let you keep doing this. It's not worth drowning over."

"I'm not drowning!"

"Yeah, well . . . your lips are purple."

Luke's eyes darted over to where I was sitting on the edge of the pool, now wringing out my hair. He glared at me under his thick eyelashes and started to argue, but Andre held up his hand.

"Besides, there's more than one way to become the kahuna," he told us. "It wasn't always a breath-holding contest, you know."

"What do you mean?" Josh asked.

Andre pointed to the lifeguard shack, which sat in the shade of a huge tree. The other lifeguards we didn't know lounged around in the shack talking. "See that big tree over there?" he said. "The first kahuna challenge started as a race from there to the volleyball courts. One year it was even a hot-dog-eating contest. Then somehow it became all about who could stay underwater the longest."

Luke looked up at Andre like his whole world had been flipped upside down. "What? Who decides all this?"

"The original kahuna."

"And who's that?" Luke asked.

Andre grinned. "Me."

Josh hefted himself out of the pool, his shorts sagging as he struggled to get out. Then he put his hands on his hips and looked up at Andre. "OK then, All Great and Powerful One. How does this kid win his title back?" He pointed to Luke. "We can't have a girl kahuna. That doesn't make any sense! She doesn't even have kahunas."

"That's not what a kahuna is," Andre said, looking down at Josh long enough to make him squirm.

Josh held up his hands. "Whoa . . . OK. Easy there, I was just kidding."

Andre continued to glare. "So you're saying my heritage is a joke?"

Josh shook his head.

Andre stared at him a beat longer, then continued. "In Hawaiian culture, a kahuna is the most respected member of the community, man or woman. People look to that person for leadership, like a wise man or a shaman."

"It's Hawaiian?" I asked. "I thought it was Polynesian?"

"That's the same thing, stupid," Josh said.

I looked closer at Andre, and suddenly I could see it. He looked like some sort of Hawaiian god, sitting on his lifeguard throne.

"That still doesn't answer my question," Josh continued. "How does Luke win his title back?"

Andre continued to look down on us from the lifeguard stand. "Let me think about it," he said. "I'll have to consult Charlie first."

"Charlie?" Josh huffed. "Why?"

"Because if it weren't for her, this whole contest wouldn't exist."

* * *

We headed back to our towels during the mandatory rest period, and as soon as we sat down, Luke, Ryan, and Josh told the others about my crash-landing on our way to the pool.

"You should have seen it!" Luke said. "She did a full-on front flip."

"It was the sickest thing I've ever seen!" Ryan added.

Josh bit into a stick of licorice. "Then that weird lady came out of her house and started yelling at us." He laughed. "You should have seen Micah's face! I thought she was going to cry."

"Yeah, thanks for pushing me down the hill!" I punched him in the arm. "I almost peed my pants." Everyone busted out laughing.

"Look at your towel." Josh used his candy to point at the wet spot where I had been sitting. "You already did."

I snagged the licorice out of his hand and took a bite.

"Hey!" he shouted.

I grinned while I chewed, enjoying the look of shock on his face as he watched me enjoy his snack.

"Gross. Didn't anybody teach you manners?" It was Trish—again. She stood over us with newly applied makeup. Megan and Ava were making their way over too.

"Come on, Trish." Megan said. She walked up and glared at her brother. "Luke, Mom said you have to go home and clean up the kitchen."

"What did I do?"

"Why don't you ask your little girlfriend?" Trish sneered, then turned on her heel.

"Ohhhh!" all the boys teased.

I felt my face turn red. "Sorry," I whispered to Luke after the girls walked away.

"It's not your fault," he mumbled.

"So she's your girlfriend, huh?" Josh taunted. He pushed Luke's head toward mine, making our foreheads clink.

"Shut up!" Luke shoved Josh's hand away. "She's not my girlfriend."

My cheeks burned even hotter now, and it had nothing to do with the heat of the day.

Luke stood up and grabbed his things. "I better go."

At that moment, Charlie blew the whistle to indicate that rest period was over. All the boys immediately jumped up and ran toward the pool, making her blow her whistle again as a warning to slow down.

I thought maybe I should go with Luke to help clean up the mess, but I didn't want the other guys to make fun of us. Instead, I chose to lie low for a minute and just sat on my towel by myself.

I looked over and saw Megan sitting in her usual spot by the pool. For once, she was alone. Just then she looked up and waved me over. I grabbed my towel, wrapping it around my waist as I went to join her.

"Did you get a new suit?" Megan asked as I walked up.

"Yeah," I said, sitting down next to her.

"It's cute." She smiled.

"Thanks." I didn't know why, but compliments like that always embarrassed me. "Where are Ava and Trish?" I asked to change the subject.

"They're in the bathroom."

I cringed. I rarely used the bathroom at pools. I hated the way the wet floors felt on my bare feet.

Before I could even think about what was coming out of my mouth I said, "They hate me, don't they?"

Megan turned to face me. "They don't hate you. They just . . . ," she trailed off.

"Hate me," I finished for her.

She looked out at the pool, trying to think of something to say.

"It's OK," I said. "But I *didn't* shake up that soda."

Megan looked away from the pool and back at me. "I know. I saw Luke throw it at you. Trish was being a jerk when she took it from you anyway." She started to giggle. "It was actually pretty funny."

I started laughing too. "Yeah, well . . ."

"She's not that bad, you know. She's actually pretty nice once you get to know her."

"Really?" I was skeptical.

Megan nodded. "We've been friends since third grade.

She wasn't always so into herself. She used to play more and be fun and stuff. But then she started to crush on Luke, and now I wonder if she's actually coming over to hang out with me or to flirt with my brother."

"What about Ava?"

"Ava and I have been best friends since kindergarten. She'll always be my best friend. But . . . I don't know. Sometimes when she's around Trish she tries to act like she's way older than she is with all her makeup and stuff."

I nodded. It made me think of Libby and the way she'd acted around Marissa and Samantha. It had made me feel left out and alone.

I looked at Megan and wondered if she ever felt like that. I doubted it. But there was something about the look on her face that told me I might be wrong.

We sat there listening to the kids giggle in the baby pool behind us for a while until Megan said, "So, I never asked, where did you move from?"

"I used to live in Wellington Estates."

Megan nodded. "Oh, that's not far then. Are you worried about missing your friends when school starts?"

I wasn't sure what to say to that, but before I could stop myself, the truth came out. "I don't really have many friends left there."

"Why?"

Thankfully, Ava and Trish saved me from answering.

"Megan! Come on!" They waved her over from where they'd tiptoed into the shallow end of the pool, and I was grateful for the interruption.

"Come with us," Megan said, nodding toward the pool.

"That's OK." I smiled at her. "I'll let Trish cool down a bit first."

"OK." Megan looked at me, hesitating.

I shouldn't have said anything. I couldn't take her feeling bad for me. "No really," I said, slipping on my flip-flops. "I've got to go home anyway."

CHAPTER 12

68 days left

I passed Josh and Ryan, along with the other boys, as I made my way toward the gated exit. They were all staring at me as I passed. It made me feel weird, so I wrapped my towel around my waist to shield myself.

"Hey! Where are you going?" Josh shouted through a muffled mouthful of candy.

"Home."

"Why?" he asked.

I didn't know what to say to that. *Because Trish keeps glaring at me through her gloppy mascara, and I secretly want to catch up with Luke to help him clean up the mess so he can brush my hair out of my face, look me in the eye, and confess his undying love to me. . . .*

Whoa . . . wait. That got weird.

"Because I want to go home," I snapped. "Why do you care?"

Josh shrugged. "We've gotta make plans to get Ryan's skateboard back. And seeing as how *you* were the one who lost it, I thought you might want to help."

"Oh . . . OK." I shrugged back. "Should we go get it now?"

"In the daylight? Are you kidding?" Josh looked at the other guys with disbelief.

"Why not?" I asked.

Josh laughed. "Why not?" he mimicked. "Did you not see what I saw? That's the creepiest house in the neighborhood. I'm not letting that lady see me in her yard." He took another bite of licorice and shook his head. "It's not worth it."

"So sneaking around her yard at night is better?" Ryan asked, drying himself off with his towel.

"Yeah."

Ryan chuckled. "OK, whatever you say. I don't know what's so creepy about it. It's just a bunch of toys."

Josh stared at him. "Exactly! Haven't you heard of Chuckie?"

Ryan ignored him and turned to me. "Mind if I walk with you? I gotta go home too."

"Sure," I said, a little taken aback.

"Hey! Where are you going?" Josh shouted. "We've gotta come up with a plan!"

Ryan ignored him and started to walk off, throwing his shirt over his shoulder.

"Meet up at the soccer field tonight at eight-thirty! Bring your flashlight!" Josh yelled at our backs. "And wear black!"

Ryan waved his hand over his head. I couldn't tell if he was dismissing Josh or waving in agreement. Apparently, Josh couldn't tell either because he shouted again, "Be there!"

* * *

The trek home with Ryan was more relaxed than I'd thought it would be. He had a quiet way about him, but it was comfortable. I didn't feel awkward at all as I walked with him, listening to our flip-flops flap in unison.

We walked in silence for a few minutes before coming up to the house where I'd lost his skateboard. We both slowed down a little to see if we could spot it under the bushes.

"I can't see anything," I said, looking harder.

Ryan ducked down next to me. "Me neither."

I studied the yard before us with the toys sprawled out all over the place. At second glance, it didn't seem as scary as I'd thought earlier. It just looked like the lady had more kids than she could handle.

Eventually Ryan and I stood up together and started walking again.

"I'm sorry I lost your board," I said, breaking the silence.

"Don't worry about it. I was going to give it to you anyway."

I looked at him in surprise. "You were? Why?"

"I don't know." Ryan looked at me. His eyes seemed darker today as they squinted at me in the shade of a pecan tree. "You looked like you needed it."

I felt myself bristle a little. "Why do you say that?"

Ryan shrugged. "Because you didn't have one. It'd be hard for you to keep up if you're going to hang out with us."

"Oh." I didn't know what else say.

We started walking again, and once more our flip-flops fell in sync. I looked over at Ryan as we walked up the hill. He kept staring forward, squinting his eyes in the blinding sunshine.

"But . . . what would *you* ride if I took your board?" I asked.

"I don't know," he said, shuffling his feet. "I'd think of something."

We came up to Luke's street. I didn't *have* to go this way to get home, but I *could*. I started to turn, but Ryan didn't come with me.

"I'm down here." He pointed up the street.

"Oh. OK," I said, trying to sound natural. "I'll see you later."

"Are you going to Luke's?" he asked point-blank.

"No," I said in a rush. Even though that was exactly where I'd been planning on going.

"Do you like him?"

"No." *Yes.* "Why?"

Ryan shrugged. "Just wondering." He turned like he was going to walk off, but then he stopped and faced me again. "Are you going to the soccer fields tonight?"

I shrugged. "I will if you will."

He smiled and nodded. "I'll see you there then."

CHAPTER 13

68 days left

I didn't end up going to Luke's house like I'd planned. For some reason, I didn't want Ryan to know that was what I had intended all along. It was a bit unnerving the way he seemed to see through me. That meant it was obvious how much I really *did* like Luke. Instead, I made my way home.

Later that night, I was sitting on the couch eating take-out Mexican food with my dad when there was a knock on the door.

"I'll get it," Dad said, licking queso from his fingers. A few minutes later I heard him say, "Micah! It's for you."

When I got to the door, I was surprised to see Megan standing on my porch wearing all black. She even had black smudges under her eyes. "Hey!" she said cheerily. "You wanna have some fun?"

"Sure." I stepped aside so she could enter. "What are you doing?" I laughed. "I mean, why are you dressed like that?"

"You'll see." She slung her purple backpack over her shoulder and walked past me into the house.

My dad studied Megan, appraising her outfit. "I like her style. It's very Rambo chic."

"What?" Megan and I both asked.

Dad shook his head. "Never mind."

Megan and I made our way back to my bedroom. The walls were still bare, but she didn't seem to notice as she plopped herself down on my green comforter.

"I like your room," she said, looking around.

"Really? There's nothing in it." I looked around with her, hoping she didn't notice the box of toys I still had, shoved in the corner. I just couldn't bring myself to get rid of them yet.

"Yeah, it's . . . simple. I mean, good simple. Not bad simple." She blushed a bit but composed herself. She walked over and looked at the calendar on the wall by my bed. "What are the numbers for?" she asked.

"They're dates?"

She laughed. "No, the other numbers. The ones you wrote."

"Oh," I looked down. "It's nothing."

Megan kept looking at me, waiting.

"It's a countdown to my birthday," I confessed.

"Your birthday is on the first day of school?"

I nodded.

"Well, that sucks. We'll have to plan something fun to make up for it."

I couldn't help but smile. That would be nice.

"So," Megan said, turning back to face me, "I've got a mission for you, if you choose to accept it."

"What is it?"

"Apparently Luke and his nerdy friends are going on a secret mission tonight. I don't know what it's about, but Luke is all decked out in black. I think this would be the perfect time to spy on them. We could scare the crap out of them."

I laughed. "I think they're going to find Ryan's skate-board. I accidentally lost it today. I'm actually supposed to go with them."

"Well, I think it's my turn to hang out with the new girl," Megan said with an evil grin. "It's not fair they get to have all the fun."

"Where are Ava and Trish?" I asked.

Megan rolled her eyes. "At the soccer field meeting up with some eighth grader Trish has been texting. She only started texting him to make Luke jealous. It's stupid. I don't know what's wrong with them. There is more to life than flirting with boys—especially my brother. They seriously have no idea how gross he really is."

"Oh." I wondered if she could tell how much I liked her brother too.

"Anyway," Megan said, changing the subject, "what time are you supposed to meet the guys?"

"Josh said to meet up at the soccer field at eight-thirty."

Megan pulled her phone out of her pocket. "It's eight-seventeen. We'd better hurry." She dug deeper into her bag. "Do you have anything black to wear?"

"Yeah, I've got one of my dad's T-shirts right here." I gestured toward the pile of clothes on the floor of my closet.

"OK, I brought you a black ski cap just in case. Your hair is like, white blond, so we have to cover it."

"OK." I grabbed the T-shirt off the floor and waited for Megan to leave—or at least turn around—but she just sat there, waiting for me to get changed.

I stood there awkwardly for a second. *How am I supposed to change shirts without her noticing I don't wear a bra?*

Ultimately I settled for pulling the black T-shirt over the shirt I was already wearing. Luckily my dad's shirt was big enough to cover me while I maneuvered my way out of the shirt I'd been wearing.

Just as I pulled my shirt out from under the oversize black T-shirt, the doorbell rang.

"Are they supposed to come get you?" Megan whispered in a panicked voice.

"No. I wonder who it is?"

She rolled her eyes. "Gee, I wonder. We've got to hurry and get out of here before they see us!"

Megan and I quickly made our way out of my bedroom. In the hallway, we ran into my dad, who was walking to the front door.

"If it's one of the boys, we're not here," Megan instructed, giving him a knowing look.

Dad pointed at her with his thumb. "I like her."

"How do we get out of here without them seeing us?" she asked.

"Use my bathroom window. The screen still needs to be replaced," he said, grinning at us. "But it *will* be replaced, so don't get any ideas."

"OK, thanks. Love you," I said.

"Be home by ten, kiddo."

"OK." I rushed passed him and into his bedroom.

Megan and I made our way through the window and into the backyard without a hitch. We were just about to go through the side gate toward the front yard when Megan grabbed my arm.

"Wait!" she whispered. "You need some of this." She unscrewed the lid of her mascara.

"What are you doing?!" I asked, backing away from her.

"I'm camouflaging you." She swiped mascara under each of my eyes, then smudged it with her thumbs. "There. It really does bring out your eyes, you know," she said, winking as she pushed me through the side gate.

As we rounded the corner, we could hear the tail end of the conversation taking place at the front door.

"Oh, OK." It was a boy's voice, sounding disappointed.

"I'll tell her you came by," I heard my dad say. "What's your name?"

"Ryan."

"OK, Ryan. See ya later, buddy."

"Bye."

Megan yanked me behind the magnolia tree that encompassed my side yard and looked over at me with wide eyes. "What's Ryan doing here?" she asked in a hushed voice.

I just shrugged.

From our hiding spot, we watched as Ryan walked down the path leading from my door to the sidewalk. We were just about to emerge from behind the tree when we heard another boy's voice.

"Hey, Ryan." It was Luke. "What are you doing here?"

"Just going to the soccer field," Ryan replied. "What are you doing?"

"Going to the field too." Luke looked in the direction of my house. "Why are you going this way? It's kind of out of your way, isn't it?"

"Oh." Ryan hesitated. "I had to do something for my grams."

"At Micah's house?" Luke asked.

"This is Micah's house?"

"Duh, you've been here before."

"Weird, I didn't remember," Ryan lied. "Why are *you* here?" he asked, turning the tables.

"I'm not here. I'm just . . . walking to the soccer field."

"But you live closer to the field than Micah does."

"Yeah, I was just delivering vegetables for my mom. You know how she is."

Megan stifled a little snort. "What a little liar."

CHAPTER 14

68 days left

Megan and I waited for the boys to get farther down the street before we followed them. We kept at a distance and hid behind parked cars and bushes whenever we thought they suspected that we were there. It was all fun and games until we got cornered by a rabid-looking Chihuahua. Luckily, Megan had a beef jerky stick in her pack.

Finally we passed the house with all the toys in front. "This is where I lost the board," I whispered, pointing across the street.

"*That's* what Josh is scared of?" Megan asked.

"Yeah, I guess so." She was right. It still didn't look that scary, even in the dark.

Megan laughed. "He's such a scaredy-cat. You just wait.

You think he's scared of that house? You should see him react to one of these." She held up an egg.

"An egg?" I asked.

"He *hates* eggs. He can't watch you crack one open without gagging. It's so funny. It's like his kryptonite."

"You're kidding."

"I'm dead serious." She giggled, tossing the egg in her palm. "He has to leave the kitchen when my mom makes breakfast. Luke told me it's because Josh's older brother once convinced him he'd get super-buff if he drank raw eggs every morning. He tried it for three days but ended up getting super-sick." She tucked the egg back in the carton, then gently placed the whole thing in her backpack and looked at me. "I won't use it unless he does something to deserve it, but it's good to have just in case." She looked at her phone to check the time. "Oh crap, we better hurry!"

When we arrived at the soccer field, we hid behind the utility shed next to the tennis courts, facing the soccer fields. We could hear the boys' voices in the distance. I silently hoped they wouldn't walk too far into the field. Otherwise we wouldn't be able to hear them anymore.

Fortunately for us, they huddled right in front of the shed. Megan and I inched into the shadows between the shed and the tennis courts, trying to get closer to the boys so we could see. But I accidentally bumped my elbow on the side of the shed, causing a hollow *thud* to ring out.

Megan and I both froze and held our breath. When the boys didn't seem to notice, we scooted a little bit closer to get a better look.

"All right, boys, glad you made it," Josh said. He inspected his army of skateboard rescuers, about five boys in all huddled together. "Dean, I'm surprised your mommy let you out this late at night."

"Shut up, Josh," bellowed the annoying kid who'd kept hogging the ball during the soccer game. I had no idea his voice was so deep. He hardly ever spoke when we were at the pool. "Besides, she's not home anyway. My brother is in charge."

That sounded really weird coming from a guy who had the voice of a teenager. I looked at the other boys, all of whom were much shorter, and wondered if maybe Dean had flunked a grade or two.

"What time is it?" Josh asked, looking over at Luke.

Luke looked at his phone. "It's past eight-thirty." Just then it dinged, distracting him with an incoming message.

"Where's Micah?" Josh asked. "She's the one who lost the board in the first place. She should be here."

Megan looked over at me and quietly giggled.

"Well, technically I think *you* lost it when you shoved her down the hill," Ryan said, running his hand through his hair.

"Whatever." Josh huffed.

"Besides, I think she's on her way." Ryan glanced around as if he expected to see me walking up any minute.

"Why do you say that?" Luke asked, looking up from his phone.

"No reason." Ryan shrugged. "It's eight-thirty, right?"

"Actually it's eight forty-six," Luke replied, looking at his phone again just in time for it to ding once more.

"Is that Trish texting you?" one of the boys asked.

"Mind your business, Garrett." Luke ignored the message and tucked his phone in his pocket instead.

"Geez, just asking." Garrett gave a shrug and a creepy sideways glance. "Not all of us have as much game as you. You could share the wealth, you know."

"Well, I guess we're going to have to do this without Micah," Josh said, sounding annoyed. "Figures. I knew she was lame all along."

"I'm pretty sure she's coming," Ryan insisted, looking around again.

"What makes you so sure of that?" Luke asked, eyeing him a little longer this time.

"She told me she was," Ryan answered, refusing to meet Luke's eyes.

"Oh yeah, Ryan here walked home with her after you left the pool." Josh nudged Luke in the rib. "Who's got game now?"

"Whatever, who cares?" Dean piped up. "Let's hurry up

and do this. I have to be back before my mom gets home at nine-thirty."

"All right, all right, everybody got flashlights?" Josh asked, taking control once again.

Everyone held up their flashlights, except for Luke, who held up his phone. It dinged again.

"You'd better tell Trish to stop texting you," Josh grumbled. "We can't have that thing constantly going off while we're sneaking around."

"Done." Luke switched his phone to silent.

"Seriously, dude, how do you do it?" creeper Garrett asked, leaning closer.

Luke just looked at him and then turned away.

* * *

Megan and I gave the boys a good head start, then followed at a safe distance. It was dark now, and the sound of the cicadas in the trees was nearly deafening.

"I really wish Trish would lay off my brother," Megan said as we walked. "You'd think as my friend she would know that there is such a thing as a code."

"A code?" I asked.

"Yeah, like a stay-away-from-my-brother kind of code." She looked at me. "You don't have any brothers or sisters, do you?"

"No."

"So you wouldn't understand. It's just a thing. Trish knows better."

"Oh," I said. I forced myself to ask the question I was dreading the answer to. "Does Luke like her back?"

"Who knows? He's such a flirt. He just likes the attention he gets from girls. He'd flirt with a tree if it had boobs."

I looked down at my chest. It didn't even jiggle a little. I was definitely lacking in that department. I looked over at Megan, who definitely wasn't, and sighed.

We were getting closer to our destination now, so Megan and I snuck up behind the cars parked in each driveway until we were next door to the house with the toys. The boys were standing in the street, hiding behind a minivan parked in front of the house.

"What do we do now?" I heard Garrett whisper a little too loudly.

"Shhhhhh!"

"I say we split up," Josh ordered. "Garrett and Dean, you look for the board on the right side of the house. Luke and I will look at the left. Ryan, you look under the bushes."

"Why do I have to look in the bushes?" Ryan asked. "They're right by the front door!"

"Because it's your board, you idiot." Josh scoffed. "I'm not risking my life for it."

Megan and I hunkered lower to the ground, stifling our giggles as the boys argued. I crept closer to the tire in front of me, getting down on my hands and knees so I could peer around it without being seen. That's when I spotted it. The skateboard was right there, under the car, nudged up against the wheel I was hiding behind.

I grabbed the board and tried to get Megan's attention to show her, but she was too busy spying on the boys to notice. They had already split up and were making their way toward the house. We could see their silhouettes as they snuck into the yard.

Josh picked up two water balloons sitting in the kiddie pool and held them to his chest. "Hey, look," he whispered, loud enough for us to hear. "I'm Megan." He squished the balloons with his hands. Before anyone could react, one of them exploded. Josh smirked. "They can't handle these man hands."

Suddenly—out of nowhere—I saw something white hurl toward Josh and bounce off his chest with a *thud*.

"OW! What the—"

Smack! Another white thing smashed into his forehead and exploded.

Josh's body lurched forward, and he gagged instantaneously. "HUUURGEH . . . oh God . . . HUUULEEAH!"

"What is it?"

"What's wrong?"

Raw egg dribbled down Josh's face, and he heaved again. "It's . . . UUUUGHAH! It's an *egg*!"

"What's going on?"

"Did he say *egg*?"

"Be quiet!" Ryan whisper-shouted in the distance. "That lady is going to come out."

It was too late. The porch light clicked on, and we could hear the door creak open. Everyone froze for a nanosecond, then scattered in different directions. Josh headed our way, gagging the whole time.

Behind the car, Megan was laughing so hard that she could hardly move. I had to pull her arm and drag her with me. Luke and Ryan caught up with us by the time we rounded the corner.

"What are you doing here?" Luke asked his sister.

"Ask him," she said, pointing to Josh.

We looked behind us and saw Josh in some random person's front yard, showering in the sprinklers. He'd scrub furiously, hunch over and gag, then scrub again with even more fervor.

"Hey, is that my board?" Ryan asked, looking at me.

"Yeah, I found it under the neighbor's car," I replied, handing it to him.

The rest of the boys made their way to us as we walked toward the high school. "You scared the crap out of us," Dean said, as he huffed out of breath.

Megan had that smirk she and her brother always seemed to wear. "That was the point."

"You hit me!" Josh's voice cracked, and his shoes squeaked as he sloshed toward us, clutching his chest where the first egg had hit him. "You hit me with an egg! You know I hate eggs. Why'd you do that?"

"Why do you think?" Megan glared him down, tossing another egg in her hand.

He shirked away.

"Take your shirt off, let us see if it's bruised." Luke reached for his shirt.

"No!" Josh squealed. "I'm fine." He sniffled.

"Are you sure?" asked Ryan.

"I said I was fine!"

"OK, dude." Ryan held up his hands.

Luke rounded on us. "Were you spying on us?"

"Duh." Megan rolled her eyes.

"We were wondering where you were," Luke said, looking directly at me. "Why didn't you show up?"

"Because *I* showed up before you and Ryan did," Megan said, wearing that crooked grin again.

Luke and Ryan looked at each other, then at us. "You saw us?" Ryan asked, darting his eyes in Luke's direction.

"I knew you went to Micah's house." Luke glared at Ryan.

Before he could say anything else, Megan chipped in, "Yeah, and you were delivering vegetables, huh?"

Ryan looked right back at Luke.

They were both acting so weird, almost like they had crushes on me or something. But that was stupid. Nobody had ever liked me before. Why would they start now?

"I can't feel my nipple," Josh whimpered, pulling at his shirt.

"Good, maybe now you'll focus on your own boobs." Megan turned away from them and headed back into the direction of the school. "I say we do a little more spying. Who wants to join?"

"I do," Garrett said, rushing a little too close onto her heels.

"Who are we going to spy on?" Luke asked.

"Trish is supposed to meet up with some eighth grader on the soccer field tonight. I think that might prove interesting."

"Are they gonna make out?" Garrett asked.

Megan looked at him in disgust, then addressed her brother. "You wanna come or not?"

Luke shrugged. "OK."

"I don't know, guys," said Dean. "What time is it?"

"It's nine-ten, you big baby," Luke said. "Your mommy won't be home for another twenty minutes."

Megan led the pack to the school, then toward the utility shed she and I had hidden behind earlier. I could hear giggling in the distance but couldn't see where it was coming from because the field was too dark. A moment later,

I spotted Ava and Trish's silhouettes from the distant streetlights. They were talking to each other while simultaneously fluffing their hair and adjusting their clothes. Even from a distance I could tell they were nervous.

"Who is she meeting?" Luke asked.

Josh punched him in the shoulder. "You jealous?"

"No, this just looks shady is all."

It did look a bit shady. There were no lights on the field, and the girls were just standing in the dark with the streetlights glowing behind them.

"Let's get a closer look," Garrett suggested.

"How?" Megan asked.

"Let's army-crawl on our bellies. They won't be able to see us in the dark."

"What are you? A professional stalker?" Megan mumbled.

We all snuck as close as we could without the girls spotting us, then crawled on our bellies until we could see them in the moonlight. A few minutes later, we heard skateboards rolling up on the asphalt behind us, and everyone froze, facedown in the grass.

Two guys dismounted their boards and made their way through the fence opening toward the girls. The guys looked big—bigger than any middle schooler I'd ever seen before.

On the field, the girls quit giggling. Trish froze for a

moment, then threw her hair over her shoulder and sauntered up to them. "You must be Brandon," she said, using her flirty voice, the same one she used on Luke. "Who's your friend?"

Brandon looked back at his friend, who hissed out a laugh, then turned back to Trish.

"This is Matt," he said. He sounded like a teenager—a for-real one. "You don't really look anything like your pictures." He looked her up and down.

Trish faltered, and the other guy, Matt, laughed. "Dude, we're talking to toddlers now?" He pointed at Trish. "What are you, like eight?"

I could see Trish continue to deflate, but then she puffed up again. "Actually, we're in seventh grade."

Ava sunk back behind Trish. She looked like she wanted to disappear.

"Oh! Well that's better!" Matt laughed, then shoved Brandon. "I can't believe this, man! We're going into high school. We can't be hanging out with little girls."

"Shut up! She looked way older in her pictures."

"I thought you said they were in eighth grade," Ava said to Trish.

"They were . . . last year."

Matt looked over at Ava and stepped closer. "I don't know, this one here, though . . . she's actually kinda cute."

Ava looked horrified, but I could see Trish bristle. "For

your information," she said. "We are *both* very mature for our age."

Megan let out a disappointed sigh. "Trish . . . don't."

"Oh yeah?" Brandon said, stepping closer to call her bluff. "How mature?"

"Very." Trish puffed her chest out and held her head high.

"Damn," Garrett whispered beside me.

My stomach churned. Garrett was enjoying this way too much. It made me feel gross. I scooted closer to Megan and felt her trembling. I reached over and grabbed the egg she was clutching in her hand before she could crush it.

"What about you?" Matt asked, stepping closer to Ava. She backed away from him.

"Don't believe us?" Trish asked, taking the attention away from Ava. She walked up to Brandon and put her arms around his neck.

Matt raised his eyebrows and smiled, then looked expectantly at Ava, who shirked away.

This didn't feel right. I didn't think Trish knew what she was getting herself into. I slowly stood up, not even knowing why. It just made me feel better to be light on my toes.

"What are you doing?" Garrett whispered.

I waved him away and saw Brandon put his hands around Trish's waist. "Prove it," he said.

There was something about the look in his eye that got

to me. Before I knew what I was doing, I had thrown the egg as hard as I could in the older boy's direction. I was aiming for Brandon, but it smacked Trish in the back of her head, making her forehead bash into his mouth.

Whoops.

"Ow!" Brandon shouted, shoving Trish away from him.

Trish clutched the back of her head and whipped around. Our eyes locked, and she looked like she wanted to murder me. My heart immediately sank with regret. All around me, the boys stood up, laughing and whooping like maniacs.

Brandon and his friend cursed as they grabbed their boards and took off, leaving Trish behind, dripping in raw egg. She shook the egg from her hands and screamed, "I can't believe you!"

Ava just stood there, looking both defeated and slightly relieved as she glanced back and forth from us to Trish.

"Trish . . . ," Megan said, making her way to her friend.

Trish's chin quivered. "No! Leave me alone!"

"Trish. Come on!"

"Go away!" She stomped off, leaving Ava alone in the dark. With nothing else to do, Ava made her way toward us.

"Are you OK?" I asked, not knowing whether I should pat her on the back or not.

Ava didn't respond.

"That was so stupid!" Megan said angrily. "What was Trish thinking?" She looked at Ava. "And why did you go with her?"

"I don't know." Ava sounded defeated. "I didn't know they were that old. I thought they were going to McNeil too, not high school."

Josh looked at Megan. "Dang, Megan! How many eggs do you have?" He eyed her nervously, still clutching his chest where he'd gotten hit before. "Is no one safe?"

Megan shook her head. "Don't look at me. That was all Micah." She pointed at me.

Josh turned to gape at me. "*You* did it?"

I could feel the rest of the boys staring at me too and refused to look up. *Oh no. They all probably hate me now.*

"Yeah." I waited for the backlash.

Josh suddenly laughed out loud and slapped me on the back. "You're killing me, Micah!" He chuckled again. "You have to be the craziest kid I know."

I laughed half-heartedly. *Yeah . . . crazy.* I wasn't so sure that was a good thing.

CHAPTER 15

67 days to go

I woke up to the sound of knocking on my window. At first it just melded into the dream I was having. The eighth graders from the night before were chasing me and had followed me home. Trish had joined their ranks and still wore the look of fury she'd had on the soccer field. I huddled in my room, trying to hide from them while they pelted my window with eggs.

Knock. Knock. Knock.

It was scary at first, because I thought they were going to bust through my window. But then it just started to get annoying.

Knock, knock, knock . . .

When are they finally going to run out of eggs? I wondered dreamily.

"Wake up!"

I sat straight up in bed, beads of sweat trickling down my back.

"Come on! Don't leave me waiting out here forever!"

I rolled over and opened the window to my left. Luke was grinning at me through the screen. "Wakey, wakey."

"Luke? What are you doing?" I wrapped the blankets tighter around me, even though the breeze outside was already warm.

Luke grinned and leaned up against the window. "I've been thinking. . . . You should come out and play soccer with me."

I blinked a few times. "What? Why?"

"Well, after you ruined Trish's date last night, there's no way she's going to want you on the girls' team. She'll do whatever she can to keep you off it, and believe me, she'll pull out all the stops."

"So?" I hoped I sounded like I didn't care, even though I kind of did. "I told you, I don't play soccer."

Luke smirked. "You're a liar. I've seen you play. You're good—really good, actually. Why'd you quit, anyway? Did you get hurt or something?"

My stomach dropped. "No." *At least not in the way you're thinking.*

I leaned away from the window, glad there was a screen between us. It was weird—part of me wondered what it would feel like to tell him. But there was no way I could do that. Then he'd know everything.

"Hey, I'm not done." Luke leaned in closer. "Listen, you'd be helping me. My parents make me go to every single one of Megan's games when I'm not playing my own. It would be in my best interest if you were on that team too."

I looked up at him, surprised. "Why?"

"Because you make things interesting." He winked. "Plus, Trish would be really ticked off if you made the team, and she's hilarious when she gets mad."

My stomach clenched at the thought of having to be on a team with Trish. Especially after I'd slammed an egg into the back of her head.

What the heck is wrong with me? Why do I do stuff like that?

Luke stared at me through the screen. "Don't make me come in there and get you," he finally said.

I sighed. "Fine." It wouldn't hurt to play a little. It didn't mean I had to try out for the team or anything. It just meant that Luke would stop asking questions.

My heart fluttered a little. . . . And I'd have an excuse to hang out with him.

"Let me brush my teeth," I said. "Meet me at the front door."

Before he could reply, I shut the window and closed my curtains, letting my head fall back on my pillow. I closed my eyes. *Why does he have to be so cute?*

There was no time to waste. I sat up quickly and swapped the T-shirt I'd slept in for a clean one, then scrambled to the bathroom. I brushed my hair as fast as I could, wiped the leftover camouflage mascara out from under my eyes, and squeezed a glob of toothpaste on my toothbrush. I shoved it in my mouth while I pulled up my shorts, then flew toward the front door.

My dad was sitting on the couch drinking coffee and reading the news on his phone before work. He looked up, surprised. "Where's the fire?"

"Luke's here," I mumbled, the toothbrush still hanging out of my mouth. I flung the door open and drooled a little as I said, "Come in."

"Well, hello there, Luke. What brings you here so early?" my dad asked, leaning back and resting his arm on the back of the couch.

"Well, sir, I'm here to train your daughter."

My dad raised his eyebrows. "Is that so?" He crossed his arms over his chest. "And what exactly are you training her to do?"

"Kick butt, sir . . . at soccer, that is. Tryouts for club team are in early August, and I think Micah has a fighting chance."

Dad shot me a surprised look. "I didn't know you were interested in playing soccer again." He sounded almost delighted now.

"I'm not," I mumbled through my toothpaste. I hadn't anticipated Luke telling my dad.

"Why not? I think Luke here has a good idea. I always thought you would regret quitting. You've always been really good at it."

I shrugged as I made my way down the hall to the bathroom to spit out my toothpaste.

"You ready?" I asked Luke when I returned, starting for the door.

"Whoa, whoa, whoa!" Dad said, jumping off the couch. "You can't train on an empty stomach." He looked at his watch. "I've got some time. How do you like your eggs, Luke?"

"Scrambled." Luke grinned, making his way to my kitchen. "With ketchup."

"Good thing Josh isn't here," I muttered.

Luke laughed.

After scarfing down two eggs and a piece of toast, I was free to go. Luke and I stepped out the door just in time to see Ryan walking up the path with two longboards, one under each arm.

He slowed when he saw Luke and me together. "Hey," he said, hesitantly.

"What are you doing?" Luke asked him.

"I brought you my longboard," Ryan said, looking at me. "I bought a new one yesterday with my lawn-mowing money after I thought we lost mine."

"Oh," I reached out for it. "Thanks!"

"What, the board I lent you the other day wasn't good enough? You've gotta take his too?" Luke teased.

"Your mom wouldn't let you give her yours anyway," Ryan said. "I heard her tell you to give it to Keaton. Besides, that's a little kid's skateboard."

Luke ignored that and grabbed the new board out of Ryan's hand to inspect it. "That's a nice board," he finally said.

"Thanks. So . . . what are *you* doing here?" Ryan asked.

"I'm here to get Micah ready for tryouts."

Ryan's face lit up. "You're going to try out for Xpress?"

"No," I said, stubbornly.

"Yes," Luke said, just as stubbornly. "Don't you think she could do it?"

Ryan nodded. "Heck yeah. When do we start?"

"Right now. Let's go to my house. My dad got me some equipment, so I can do strength and agility training. We can do that before we scrimmage."

The boys walked together on the way to Luke's house. I attempted to use Ryan's old skateboard but kept falling off. At one point they each tried to hold one of my arms like they'd done before, but I wouldn't let them.

"Oh no you don't! Last time that happened I face-planted into a kiddie pool."

Luke laughed. "With style, I might add."

"Besides, it was Josh who pushed you, not us, and he's not here," Ryan said, just as we were passing Josh's house. He looked at Luke. "Should we invite him?"

"Nah . . . he's probably still sleeping."

Just then Josh bolted out of his front door. He was running toward us with his shirt over his head, arms flailing as he tried to find the right armhole.

"Wait!" His voice was muffled by the waffle hanging out of his mouth. "Where are y'all going?"

Beside me, I heard Luke sigh.

"Hey, is that your board, Ryan?" Josh asked, noticing what I was standing on. He shook his head. "You are both *suckers*! You know that?"

CHAPTER 16

5 5 days left

Nearly two weeks passed, and every day was the same. Luke would show up at my window each morning when the sun rose, so I started getting up early to brush my teeth and my hair before he arrived. Dad would make us eggs before he went to work and we met up with Josh and Ryan. Then we'd do strength and agility training at Luke's house before meeting the rest of boys at the soccer field to scrimmage. We always ended up red-faced and sweaty, and when we couldn't take the heat anymore, we headed for the pool to cool down.

Even though training was exhausting, Luke and the boys were never too tired to crowd around the lifeguard hut and harass Andre about a new kahuna challenge.

They checked in with him nearly every day. Luke was desperate to win back his title, but every day Andre insisted they had to wait a bit longer.

I hadn't seen much of Ava and Trish since the egg incident—I'd been doing my best to avoid them—but on this particular afternoon, I somehow found myself sitting with them and Megan during rest period. As usual, the girls were decked out in bikinis and makeup while I sat there dripping water all over my towel. My hair had started to dry into a crusty chlorine helmet, and I could feel Trish darting glares in my direction. I couldn't wait for Charlie to hurry up and blow the whistle.

Ava nudged Trish with her shoulder. "So . . . have you heard any more from Luke about the carnival coming up?"

Trish's eyes fell on mine. "Oh yeah, we text *all* the time."

Megan rolled her eyes and gave me a pointed look that clearly said, *Stay-away-from-my-brother code. She just doesn't get it.* But with her mouth she said, "What time is it? I need to be home by three. I'm getting my braces today." She grimaced.

"Two-fifteen," Ava said, not bothering to look up from her phone.

"Ugh. I better go," Megan said. "I'll see you guys later."

To my horror, she grabbed all her stuff and left me alone with Ava and Trish. It was the last thing I wanted. Ava seemed nice enough most of the time, but Trish made me seriously uncomfortable. I didn't want to make it obvious that I didn't want to be there, so I just sat on my towel, studying my toenails and wondering if Trish would accept my apology if I tried to give her one.

How do I even start?

Just then the whistle blew. *Finally!*

I was about to bolt up when I heard a bunch of screaming coming from behind me. It was all the boys, sprinting across the grass in our direction.

Trish and Ava giggled and squealed, pretending to cover themselves with their towels. The next thing I knew, there were a million hands on me, and I was being carried in the direction of the pool. I thought they were going to throw me in, but instead, they set me down at the foot of the lifeguard's chair.

"There you go, Micah," Luke said. "It's time."

"Time for what?"

"Time for you to prove that you actually are the kahuna. That it wasn't just a fluke."

"Yeah," Joshed popped in. "Andre is ready to tell us what the next challenge is."

"So, what is it?" I asked, looking up at Andre. I could see my distorted reflection in his sunglasses. I looked like an Oompa Loompa.

Andre looked over at Charlie, who was on duty across the pool, and smiled. Then he looked down at us. "All right,

Luke, Micah, this is between the two of you. Whoever does the best dive off the high dive gets to keep the title."

I looked up at the high dive towering above me. I didn't even like jumping off that thing feetfirst. There was no way I wanted to plummet off it headfirst.

"Look, she's scared," Josh taunted.

"No, I'm not!" I lied.

Luke grinned. "All right then, Big Kahuna." He gestured toward the ladder. "Ladies first."

I didn't move. It was like my feet had melted into the concrete. It didn't help that a crowd was beginning to gather by the edge of the pool, Ava and Trish included.

"I mean . . . you don't have to do it," Luke taunted, giving me that teasing grin of his. "Not everyone has what it takes to be the kahuna. If you don't want to prove you're worthy, that's fine."

I stepped past him and toward the high dive, refusing to let myself look Luke in the eye. *He's so infuriating . . . and beautiful. Infuriatingly beautiful.*

I stood at the bottom of the ladder and looked up. Then I heaved a sigh and slowly started climbing. I could hear the boys below me start to cheer.

"That's my girl!" Josh shouted.

I glanced back and saw Trish wrinkle her nose. "Your girl?"

"What? You jealous?" Josh gestured to Ryan. "He's my

boy." He pointed to Luke. "He's my boy." Then he pointed at me, clutching the rungs of the ladder. "And that's our girl over there."

Trish rolled her eyes, but Josh looked over at me and grinned. "Ain't that right, Micah?"

I laughed, feeling my heart squeeze a little. Josh wasn't so bad once he warmed up. "Yeah, that's right."

Trish rolled her eyes again and moved to where Ava was standing.

I smiled to myself as I continued to climb, one rung at a time. Maybe it wasn't so scary after all. I could hear the boys below me cheer again and then start to chant my name. "Micah, Micah, Micah . . ."

I looked down, which was a big mistake. I gripped the railing harder. *Never mind. Still terrifying.*

By now, even more kids had made their way to the pool to see what was going on.

"Come on, Micah! You can do it!" I heard a little voice say as I climbed the ladder.

I glanced down quickly and spotted Keaton looking up at me through his goggles, his nose positioned in its usual pig snout. He gave me the most sincere thumbs-up. I tried to give him one back, but it was brief because I didn't want to fall to my death.

By the time I got to the top of the ladder, my legs were shaking. I thought I might even pee a little. I slowly made my way across the board, gliding my hands along the metal railing as I went. When the railing ended, I hesitated to go any farther.

"Come on, Micah!" some of the boys encouraged me.

I edged closer to the end of the board, feeling it bounce a bit under my weight. It looked much higher up here than it had on the ground.

Over at the lifeguard station, Charlie sat twirling her lifeguard whistle in one hand and smiling up at me. "You've got this, Micah!" she shouted, shielding her eyes from the sun with her other hand. "Show these little punks what you're made of."

Andre was standing right next to her now, watching closely. The reflection of the pool gleamed off his sunglasses as he grinned and hollered, "Hold your arms like this!" He demonstrated how to put my arms overhead in a diving stance.

I did as he said, wobbling a bit.

"Now lean forward and lead with your head!" Andre called to me. "Keep your legs straight and stay as stiff as a board."

I looked down again at the kids watching. Trish was whispering something into Ava's ear. People were still chanting my name: "Micah! Micah! Micah!" Kids I didn't even know had now joined in.

"You can do it!" Charlie encouraged me.

I wasn't so sure about that, but I was here now. I either needed to go off the high dive or climb back down, which somehow seemed just as scary.

I took a deep breath and shook my hands out. It was probably best to just get it over with. I held my arms up overhead like Andre had shown me, then I squeezed my eyes shut and leaned forward. My toes left the board, and my stomach turned as I fell.

It seemed to take forever for the fall to be over, but as soon as I hit the water, I knew I had slightly over-rotated. My back and butt stung immediately, and the breath was knocked out of me. I could feel my butt cheeks hanging out of my bathing suit and pulled my bottoms back up as fast as I could, hoping nobody had noticed.

When I popped up I heard the chorus of, "Ohhhh!"

Andre leaned over the pool and offered to give me a hand up. "You all right?" he asked as I scrambled out.

I nodded, not quite able to breathe yet.

"She's tough as nails." Andre laughed, looking up at Charlie. "She reminds me of you."

Charlie smiled down at me. "Give 'em hell, Micah."

Andre looked over at Luke. "OK, chief, your turn."

"What?"

"You want the kahuna title back? You go."

Luke looked up at the board, then at me, and winked. "Nah, she can have it."

What?!

Andre smiled at him and then at Charlie, who in turn grinned at me.

"Holy crap that was epic! Maybe Micah does have kahunas!" Josh shouted, racing over. "Did you hear her hit the water? *SPLAT!*"

"She totally lost her bottoms," I could hear Trish say over the crowd.

I looked up at Charlie, who rolled her eyes, and I couldn't help but smile back at her.

"You did?" Luke asked.

"Totally," I admitted.

"Oh man!" He laughed and clapped me on my already sore back, causing me to wince. "Sorry," he said, leading me back to where we had left our towels.

Sensing the excitement was over, most of the other kids went back to swimming. Ava and Trish decided upon the nonswimming option—of course—and followed Luke and me toward the towels.

"Oh my gawd! Her butt is so red." Trish snickered as she walked behind us.

"How bad did it look?" I asked Luke.

"How bad did it feel?"

"Pretty bad."

He laughed. "Yeah, that's how it looked. That's why I didn't do it." I must have been scowling as I went to sit on my towel, because Luke held up his hands. "Hey! Don't look at me like that. Now it's official."

"What's official?"

Luke plopped down on my towel with me. "You're the kahuna. And you're one of us." He grinned again. "You're our girl."

I liked the sound of that. Luke draped his arm around my shoulder, and I could feel the sun radiating off his skin and onto my own. My heart was thudding faster and faster. It was almost as if with each pump my heart said, *I. Like. Luke. I. Like. Luke.*

"So what time are we meeting up on the field?" Trish interrupted, sitting across from us. Her eyes flickered from Luke to me and then back to Luke.

"What?"

"The Fourth of July? You know, Monday . . ." She looked at him expectantly, but Luke's face was still blank, like he didn't know what she was talking about. Trish looked at Ava for backup, but Ava was too busy scrolling through her phone to notice.

"You asked me to watch the fireworks with you?" Trish continued. "It's less than a week away, and we still haven't finalized our plans."

"Oh. That." Luke took his arm off my shoulder, looking uncomfortable.

I had totally forgotten that Trish had plans to meet up

with Luke on the Fourth. It seemed like forever ago that I'd sat next to her, in this exact spot, listening to her brag about it.

I looked at Luke, who was looking back at Trish, and it suddenly became blatantly clear to me. He would never like me the way I liked him. How could he? Boys like him didn't like girls like me. They liked girls like Trish.

Luke was just a flirty boy who liked to flirt with flirty girls. I was one of the boys, the kahuna, and Trish was a girly girl—the kind of girl boys wanted to kiss on soccer fields while fireworks exploded in the sky.

My eyes started to water, and panic rose in my chest as I tried to ignore the rest of the conversation that was taking place next to me. There was no way I could let Luke or Trish know how I was feeling.

Luke probably already knows I'm in love with him and doesn't want to hurt my feelings, I thought.

I didn't want to blink because I didn't want the tears to spill over, so I just stared in the general direction of the pool. The rest of the boys were sitting on the edge, but I wasn't really looking at them. I wasn't really looking at anything. I was just concentrating on not crying.

"Who are you staring at?" Luke asked me suddenly.

"Oh my gawd. She's looking at Ryan," Trish said with a smile.

"No I'm not!" I protested.

"Yes, you are! You are totally crushing on him, aren't you?"

"You like Ryan?" Luke asked, looking at me hard.

"No! I don't like anyone," I lied.

Just then Ryan saw us all looking in his direction and started to make his way toward us.

Oh no. No, no, no. Stop. Turn around.

"Well here's your chance, Micah," Luke said, nudging me in the ribs. "Ask him to watch the fireworks with you."

I could hear the challenge in his voice. *What is he doing?*

"Yeah, Micah, I've seen him looking at you before," Trish said, darting her eyes in Luke's direction, then over at me. The smile on her face was as fake as they came. "Haven't you seen it, Ava?"

"What?" Ava asked, briefly looking up from her phone.

"Don't you think Micah and Ryan would make a cute couple?"

Ava shrugged. "I don't know. I've never really thought about it." She looked at me closer.

"Oh my gosh, you're blushing!" Trish said.

"No, I'm not!"

"Ava! Isn't this the cutest thing ever?! Micah is, like, so in love with Ryan."

Luke was looking at me hard, as if he were trying to decipher whether or not I was blushing. I could feel the tears build up again. I had to get out of there. I stood up abruptly, grabbing my towel and longboard.

"He's the one who gave you that board, wasn't he?" Ava asked. "How sweet! He must really like you too."

I froze. I'd been planning on riding the board home to escape this mess, but I couldn't do that now or it would make what Trish had said true. Instead, I just dropped it and let the board clatter behind me on the concrete as I walked off as fast as I could.

CHAPTER 17

55 days left

I had almost made it out the exit when someone called my name from the direction of the lifeguard hut. "Micah! Wait up."

Tears were streaming down my face now. I didn't want anyone to see me crying, so I ducked my head and plowed on.

"Wait!" It was Charlie. She caught up to me and grabbed me by the shoulders, turning me to face her. "What's wrong? Did you get hurt on the high dive?"

I shook my head, darting a glance toward where Trish still sat with Luke and Ryan.

Charlie caught where I was looking and sighed. "Come here. Come inside with me." She ushered me toward the lifeguard hut, past the counter where Andre and another guy were stationed. "Andre, could you get Destiny to cover the concession stand for me? Or maybe Jordan?"

He looked over at me with concern on his face. "Sure. Did Micah get hurt?"

"We just need to have some girl talk, is all."

Charlie led me deeper into the lifeguard's hut and past the concession stand. "Do you want anything?" she asked, gesturing to the freezer where the Popsicles and frozen candy bars were kept.

I shook my head again, but Charlie grabbed a candy bar anyway and led me through another doorway that went outside again. We were at the back of the building now, where none of the swimmers ever went. There were a few lawn chairs and a mini table covered with empty fast-food cups, sitting in the shade of a huge tree. Apparently this was where the lifeguards went when they wanted a break.

Charlie gestured for me to take a seat in one of the chairs. "So . . . let me guess. Mean-girl trouble?"

I looked up at her. "Kind of."

Charlie leaned back in her chair, unwrapped the candy bar, and handed it to me. "She's jealous, you know."

I barked out a laugh and bit into the candy. "Sure," I said, chewing slowly.

"Believe me, as a lifeguard it's my job to sit and stare

at people all day. Hardly anybody ever drowns, so I have no choice but to people watch. And I'm telling you, Trish is jealous."

I looked down at the candy bar, twirling it in my hand and rubbing the condensation off the frozen chocolate. I could feel Charlie looking at me.

"You really do remind me of me when I was your age," she said.

I looked up at Charlie's dark eyes and tan skin. Her curly hair was up in its usual ponytail on the top of her head. We looked nothing alike.

"I was kind of a tomboy too," she said smiling at me. "Do you know what I like about you, Micah?"

"What?"

"That you're just *you*. You don't try too hard like some of the other girls out there. You're authentic. I think that's why you have such a fan club."

"A fan club?"

She smiled. "All those boys out there?"

I shook my head. "I'm just one of the boys. They don't look at me like they look at the other girls."

"They will," a voice said from behind me. I turned to see Andre making his way toward us. "You just wait, Micah." He smiled at Charlie.

"Should we show her?" she asked him.

"I mean . . . she *is* the reigning kahuna," Andre replied.

"I think she deserves to know." He held out his hand and pulled me out of my chair.

"Show me what?" I asked.

"It's kind of nerdy, so don't judge us," Andre said.

I followed them around the big tree shading us. On the back of the tree, two letters—C and A—had been carved into the wood. Tally marks were slashed underneath.

"This is where it all began," Andre said, pointing to the carvings. "Charlie versus Andre."

"We were in fifth grade when it started," Charlie continued. "I had just moved here from South Carolina and had no friends. Back then the cool thing to do was race from that fence to the volleyball court and back to see who was the fastest."

"I was always the fastest," Andre said, joining in. "Then one day this cute girl showed up at the pool and asked if she could race. Long story short, she kicked my butt, and I got super-embarrassed. Out of anger I said some things that I shouldn't have."

I looked at him. I knew how that went.

"I didn't come back to the pool for weeks," Charlie said. "I didn't want to come back ever."

"I felt really bad about it," Andre said. "I knew where she lived because my grandma lived next door to her and had mentioned when Charlie moved in. So one day I went over to Charlie's house and challenged her for the title of kahuna." He laughed. "I just wanted a reason to talk to her, but I got the idea from my grandma, who'd told me about the different types of kahunas in our culture. In Hawaii there are kahunas for things like medicine, agriculture. . . . Anyway, I thought it would be kind of cool to play up that part of me to impress Charlie, so I went over to her house one day and issued the challenge."

Charlie smiled at him. "So, I heard a knock at the door and looked out the window to see Andre standing there. I was still really mad at him, so I made my big brother answer it."

"The guy still scares me to this day."

Charlie giggled. "Andre challenged me to compete for that stupid title, and I took it on because I wanted to beat him. I wanted to embarrass him just as badly as he'd embarrassed me. From then on, we challenged for everything. You name it, we did it. And we tallied it up here on this tree."

"Over time we became friends, even though I really wanted her to be my girlfriend." Andre grinned. "It took me years to work up the courage to tell her that I liked her."

Charlie sighed. "This is our last summer here together." She suddenly looked like she might cry.

Andre put his arm around her. "I'm joining the Navy, and this little rock star here got a scholarship to play soccer for Midwestern State, so she'll be sticking around."

Charlie tried to smile, but I could tell it wasn't quite working. I looked at the two of them as Andre pulled her in closer. Then I looked at the tree with the carvings. I wondered what it would feel like to have a boy like me that much. Enough to make up a challenge just so he could be around me.

"When you walked in here that first day, you immediately reminded me of Charlie the first time I met her," Andre said to me. "You've got the same grit."

I looked over at Charlie. I wished I *were* like her. She was everything I wanted to be.

Just then the fence rattled on the other side of the bushes, and skateboards clattered onto the cement. "What happened to Micah? Where'd she go?" a boy's voice asked from the other side. It sounded like Ryan.

Both Charlie and Andre looked over at me and smiled.

"I don't know. She just took off," another familiar voice replied. It was Luke.

"What'd you say to her, Luke?"

"I didn't say anything!"

"You promised you wouldn't tell anyone."

"I didn't! But it's pretty obvious you like her, dude."

"Yeah, well it looks like you like her too," Ryan said.

"I told you I didn't, so drop it!" Luke snapped. A moment later, we heard the boys skate away.

I looked up to see Charlie and Andre still grinning at me.

"See?" Andre gave me a gentle punch on the shoulder. "Now let's hope they're smart enough to figure some things out sooner than I did."

CHAPTER 18

54 days left

I woke up earlier than usual the next day. I couldn't stop thinking about Ryan and Luke. After they'd left, I had gone back to grab my skateboard, and the whole ride home I thought about what I'd overheard. I didn't know what to make of it all. I wanted to talk to somebody about it, but I didn't know who. I couldn't talk to Dad. He'd just get all weird and start talking about gardening equipment. And I couldn't talk to Megan because she had that whole stay-away-from-my-brother code.

The person I needed was my mom. She'd know what to think of it all. I had always hoped the dull ache from missing her would fade, but it seemed the older I got, the worse it became. I needed her now more than ever.

I lay in bed for a moment longer, listening to the birds

chirping in the magnolia tree outside my open window. The waxy blossoms had been Mom's favorite flower. Every time we'd passed a magnolia tree, she'd point it out and ask, "What do you think, Micah? What are the magnolias going to smell like today?"

I'd always thought that was dumb—to me they'd always smelled the same—but suddenly, I was curious. Maybe they *would* smell different today.

It was still cool outside when I stepped into the yard. The sun was just beginning to glint off the drops of morning dew spread throughout the yard, and the little beads of water clung to the grass and the bottoms of my feet as I walked toward the tree.

When I looked closer at the tiny drops, I saw little rainbows reflecting inside each one, like hidden secrets. That was the type of thing Mom would have noticed and then filed away in her memory to draw later. Seeing it made me miss her even more.

The closer I got, the louder the birds sang, almost like they were greeting me. They seemed to watch curiously as I walked around smelling every blossom I could reach, trying to decide how I would describe it to Mom if she were here.

To me, the different blossoms smelled like Mom and her different moods. Some were playful and so lemony-good that I wanted to eat them, while others held the lingering scent of sunshine, like a warm hug on a summer day. And then there were the few stormy flowers that seemed to shadow the rest. They reminded me of the way the air smelled when dark clouds rolled in before a tornado or a torrential rain.

Suddenly, among the thick leaves of the magnolia tree, I could feel her around me. Like I could talk to her here in the branches, and she would be there to listen. There was no one else around, so that's what I did.

I climbed the limbs, and once I was high enough, I told her about my summer so far—about the friends I had made and the embarrassing things I had done. Then I told her about the conversation I'd overheard between Luke and Ryan and what it could possibly mean.

As I spoke, the birds stopped chirping. It was almost like they were listening too.

* * *

By the time I returned to the pool, things had gone back to normal with the boys. So normal in fact, that a part of me wondered if I had imagined the whole conversation between Luke and Ryan.

It was particularly hot and humid that day—one of those days where the sky wasn't even blue anymore but a stark white, and I felt sweaty and sticky, even though I had just gotten out of the pool.

My thighs felt like they were rubbing together even more than usual as Megan and I made our way back to our towels. "Where are Ava and Trish?" I asked, handing her one of the candy bars I'd just bought.

"Ava went to California to see her aunt, and Trish is at some fancy soccer camp with her new friends," Megan replied.

Something about her voice made me look up. She seemed sad.

Megan saw me looking and shrugged it off. "I just haven't seen her much lately. She's been hanging out with her new friends a lot."

I nodded. I knew that feeling. It wasn't a good one.

As we walked across the hot cement, I caught sight of the boys hanging out by the lifeguard stand talking to Andre. Luke caught me watching him and winked. I darted my eyes over at Megan, but she was too busy fixing her towel to notice.

I bent down to readjust my towel too and heard Megan gasp from behind me.

"What?" I straightened up.

"Micah!" Megan whispered urgently. "I think you started your period."

I blinked. "What? I don't have periods."

"I think you do now," she said, pointing to my legs.

I looked down to see a faint pink strip dripping down

my leg. I just stared at it. *This can't be happening.*

"Oh crap, the boys are coming," Megan said. "Quick! Wrap your towel around your waist."

I did as she said and hurriedly started gathering my stuff. I had to get out of here.

Just then the boys arrived. "Where are you going?" Luke asked.

"None of your business!" Megan shouted at him, grabbing her stuff too.

I darted off without looking him—or any of the other boys—in the eye. Megan was right behind me. There was no way I was going to let them know what was going on.

"Do you have pads at your house?" Megan asked as we scurried through the pool exit.

"No." I could feel the threat of tears build up in my eyes.

Megan put her arm around my shoulder. "Come on, we can go to my house."

The walk was torturous. I was terrified I was going to leave a trail of blood on the sidewalk, so I put my towel between my legs, making a makeshift diaper. Megan helped me tie the towel at the sides.

"I look like a baby!" I cried, not sure if I was really crying or laughing.

"No, you don't," she said. "More like a sumo wrestler."

I snort-laughed. "My thighs are chafing. Let's hurry this up. I can't stand the way this feels."

We walked a little bit faster. Well, Megan walked. I waddled. We were almost to her house when I heard a bunch of skateboards rolling up behind us.

"Hurry!" Megan pushed me into her front yard.

I gave up on my towel-diaper, wadding it up under my arm and running to the door. A wave of cool air hit my face as we rushed in. Megan slammed the door behind us and locked it.

"Go to the bathroom!" she ordered. "I'll meet you there."

My bare feet were firmly planted on the cold tile floor, frozen with panic. I jumped when I heard banging on the door behind me.

"Megan! Let us in!"

"Mom!" Megan called. "Don't let the boys in! Micah just got her period, and they're following us!"

Sandi looked up from the book she was reading on the couch. "What?"

"Micah started her period for the first time!" Megan shouted.

I winced. I wished she'd be a little quieter about it.

"You have to distract them!" Megan said, darting to the back door and locking it. Then she rushed into the kitchen and toward the garage door that led into it. She was about to lock that too when someone started turning the handle from the other side.

"Micah! What are you doing? Go!" Megan wrestled with the handle but ultimately won and locked it.

More banging came. "MOM! Megan locked us out! It's hot out here!"

"Over here." Megan ushered me to her bedroom. I had never been in there before. Unlike Luke's room, Megan's was perfectly organized. She'd even made her bed.

"Here, you can use my bathroom. Lock the other door, though; it leads to Luke's room. I'll get you something to change into."

What am I going to wear? I thought, panicked. *I don't have any underwear!*

"My mom bought me some new underwear yesterday. You can keep these," Megan said, reading my mind. She handed me a stack of clothes. "Oh, and there are pads and tampons under the sink."

I heard the door clink shut behind her, and I just stood there for a minute. *Tampons?! There's no way that's happening.*

I looked over to the door that led into Luke's room and locked it. Almost immediately I heard someone try the handle.

"What the—" *BAM!* Someone hit the door. "MOM! She locked me out of my own bathroom! I have to pee!"

I faintly heard Sandi tell Luke to use her bathroom.

Shaking, I stood there for a minute to make sure he was gone. There was no way I was taking off my bloody bathing suit with him on the other side of the door. Once it was quiet enough that I was sure he'd left, I grabbed a pad from under the sink and turned it over in my hand, studying it. It looked like a weird puberty diaper.

The pile of clothing Megan had given me included a black bra. I was sure there was no way I'd fill that sucker out, but I decided to give it a shot anyway to see how it fit. Surprisingly, it wasn't all that loose. It was heavily padded and made my boobs look ten times bigger than they actually were.

Whoa . . . is this why Megan and all her friends look like they have actual boobs?

I pulled the light-blue tank top Megan had given me over my head and was admiring my new shapely figure in the mirror when I heard voices on the other side of Luke's door.

"What is their problem?" he asked. "She was our friend first."

I looked down at my bathing suit, now crumpled up on the floor. I had to get rid of it before the boys saw it.

So much for my new suit, I thought.

Suddenly the need for my mom swelled up in my chest. I missed her now more than ever. But there was no time to dwell on what I couldn't have. I had to hide my ruined swimsuit. I quickly pulled on Megan's jean shorts and snatched my suit off the floor before walking back through the door to her room.

"I knew that color would look good on you," Megan said, nodding to the tank top I was wearing. "It brings out the blue in your eyes . . . and your tan."

"Thanks." I looked down, embarrassed. I wadded up the damp bathing suit in my hands even tighter, trying to cover the bottoms with the top.

Megan motioned toward it. "We can give that to my mom. I'm sure she'll wash it for you. But I think she's going to take us shopping first," she said.

"For what?"

"Pads, of course." Megan looked at me thoughtfully for a minute, as if she were carefully choosing what she said next. "Luke told us."

"Told you what?"

She hesitated a bit. "About your mom."

"Oh."

"I can't imagine asking my dad to buy me pads. I would be so embarrassed. So my mom and I thought we should go get you some."

"Oh," I said again. I swallowed the lump that was beginning to form in my throat. It should have been *my* mom taking me shopping.

Just then it dawned on me. I was going to have to tell my dad. I started to get a bad feeling in my gut—the strange, hollow kind of feeling you get when you're homesick. Everything felt weird now. Nothing was ever going to be the same.

I could feel hot tears well up, but I blinked them back. I hated it when things changed like this, so suddenly. You'd think I'd be used to it by now. But change was like that—always unexpected, impossible to see coming.

CHAPTER 19

54 days left

Getting out of the house without the boys seeing us proved tricky. We'd nearly made it to the garage without being spotted when Megan's little brother, Keaton, gave us away.

"Hey! Where are you going?" he asked loudly, blocking our way.

"Nowhere. Don't worry about it," Megan said, pushing past him.

"I want to go!"

"You can't go with us, Keaton!"

"Why not?!"

"You just can't! Mom! Hurry up!"

"*MOM!* I want to go!" Keaton whined.

"Honey, you can't go on this trip," Sandi said, giving

him a quick kiss on his forehead before grabbing her purse off the kitchen counter.

"But I want to! I'm bored!"

"Where are you going?" Luke asked as he walked into the kitchen. His eyes met mine, but I looked away. This was all too embarrassing to handle.

"We're just making a quick girls' trip," Sandi said, flashing me a wink so fast I wasn't sure if it had actually happened.

So that's where Luke gets it.

"Whatever." Luke gave me a hurt look before he turned his back on me and headed to his room. I felt a knot form in my stomach.

"Watch your brother while we're gone!" Sandi called after him.

He didn't even acknowledge her.

* * *

I thought the trip to the store would be awkward, but I felt strangely at ease as I sat in the back seat of Sandi's SUV. She rolled down all the windows and blared an old song I had never heard.

"Oh! I love this song!" Sandi exclaimed. She turned up the volume so that a guitar riff blasted through the speakers. "I love Gwen Stefani! She reminds me of college."

Megan and I exchanged glances. Megan rolled her eyes,

but I giggled as Sandi belted, *"'Cause I'm just a girl I'd rather not be . . . ohhhh! I've had it up to here!"*

It was the best song I'd ever heard. It made me wish I knew how to play the guitar, because I was dying to play that riff. We were all laughing and windblown by the time we pulled up to the drugstore parking lot.

After navigating the pad department—*if that's what you call it*—Sandi led us to the junk-food aisle.

"Ladies," she said, all businesslike, "I can't help but feel that this occasion calls for some junk food and a sleepover. I have the perfect movie for you to watch. It's another one of my favorites."

Again, Megan rolled her eyes, but I could see a smile lingering at the corners of her mouth.

"What do you say, Micah? Do you think your dad will let you stay over?" Sandi asked.

"Probably." I grinned at her. "I can ask."

"Here, use my phone," she said, digging in her purse. "And you can each pick out two snacks. I'm going to pick something up for the boys, so they don't throw a fit."

My dad insisted on coming over to meet Sandi and her husband before granting permission. I was embarrassed, but Sandi didn't seem bothered by it at all. In fact, she asked to speak to him and ended up inviting him over for dinner as well.

"We can just go ahead and have our little cookout

tonight, if you're available," she said cheerily through the phone.

I wasn't sure what Dad said on the other end, but by the time Sandi hung up the phone, plans were made.

"Well, that settles that." She smiled and pointed to the junk food Megan and I were clutching in our hands. "Put that stuff back. We'll get your snacks at the grocery store. I've got to get stuff for a cookout."

* * *

When we got back to the house, Keaton greeted us at the door. Luke was still in his room and didn't bother to come out.

My dad was supposed to be there any minute, and I felt nervous for some reason. Would he be able to tell that there was something different about me since I started my period?

My mind drifted to Mom again. If she were here, Dad wouldn't even need to know what was going on. We could both pretend like nothing had changed.

I went into Megan's bathroom and looked in the mirror. I was certain my new padded boobs would give me away, so I slipped off the bra. My budding boobies stared at me through the thin tank top I was wearing, so I slipped the bra back on with a sigh. Then I made my way back to the kitchen, where Megan was helping her mom cut up zucchini for grilling.

"Why do you grow so much of this stuff?" Megan was asking.

"Because it makes me feel like a successful gardener."

"Well, nobody likes it."

"Oh really?" Sandi shot her daughter a look. "How did you like those muffins I made for you the other day?"

"They were OK, I guess," Megan said, doubtfully.

"Guess what was in them?"

"Seriously?" Megan said. "You put zucchini in our muffins?"

"Eew!" Keaton screeched around a mouthful of potato chips. "You have to warn us before you feed us vegetables."

"That would defeat the purpose, my dear," Sandi said, turning back around to face the counter. She snagged the bag out of Keaton's hands and put it on top of the refrigerator. "Get out of those!"

Just then the doorbell rang.

"I've got it!" Keaton screeched.

"Too late." Luke came out of nowhere and stiff-armed his little brother in the forehead, making him fall on his butt.

Luke opened the door. "Oh. It's just Dad."

"Why is the door locked?" Luke's dad asked as he came inside. He was even more handsome than in the pictures I'd seen around the house and seemed taller in person. His face lit up when he smiled at Sandi.

Luke glared at Megan and me instead of answering.

Sandi gave her husband a kiss. "Why are you going through the front door?"

"I think my garage-door opener needs a new battery," he replied. Then he looked up at me and smiled. "You must be Micah. I've heard a lot about you." He ruffled Luke's hair and gave him a look.

Luke swatted his dad's hand away and walked back to his room.

"Where are you going?" his dad asked.

"Where does it look like?" Luke retorted. He hesitated when his dad gave him a warning look. "To my room," he corrected.

Sandi and her husband had a quick eyeball conversation that I couldn't decipher, then she said, "Long story." She turned to me. "Micah, this is Nick."

Nick reached out for me to shake his hand. I put my limp hand in his. "Nice to meet you," I said shyly.

"Likewise." He flashed me another smile, then reached into the fridge to grab a beer. "So, what's for dinner?"

Megan held up the massive zucchini she was in the middle of chopping.

"Again?" Nick asked, twisting the cap off his bottle.

Sandi pointed the tongs in his direction. "I don't want to hear it! Not from you, too," she warned. Nick chuckled and gave her another kiss on the cheek.

Just then the doorbell rang again. "I got it!" Keaton shouted.

"Nope," said Luke, reappearing once again. Keaton didn't even bother running over this time.

"Hi, Luke," I heard my dad say.

"Come on in," Luke said, stepping aside.

Luke's dad walked up for a handshake. "Hi, I'm Nick Waters."

Waters, I repeated silently. *Luke Waters.* It struck me that I hadn't even known what the twins' last name was until then.

"Brent McKinney," my dad replied, grabbing Nick's hand. I could tell he was trying to be manly too, even though Nick towered over him.

"You wanna beer?" Nick offered, motioning to the bottle he held.

"Sure." My dad rubbed his hands on his jeans, a nervous habit of his.

"Hey, Dad," I said from the kitchen.

"Hey, kiddo. You overstaying your welcome?"

"Never." Sandi smiled with her sparkly sea-green eyes. "She's welcome anytime. I'm Sandi." She held up her hands to show that they were covered in hamburger meat. "We're so glad y'all could stay for dinner."

It didn't take long for my dad and Nick to find their way to the backyard, where they sat on the patio drinking beer.

NINA CHAPMAN

"Your dad is handsome, Micah," Sandi said.

"Mom, you're so weird." Luke snagged the bag of chips off the top of the refrigerator.

"What? Micah's a pretty girl too. It would do you good to show you have manners."

"*MOM!*"

"Look, he's blushing," Sandi said, giving me another wink.

Luke took the bag of chips into his room and slammed his door.

* * *

Dinner was served under a huge red umbrella on the Waters's patio. I had just taken a bite out of my burger, squirting a big glob of ketchup onto my shirt—well, Megan's shirt—when I caught Luke looking at me from across the table.

"So," Nick said, wiping his mouth with a napkin, "how was everyone's day?"

"Micah got a period," Keaton announced, biting into his corn on the cob as if that were a normal thing to say.

My dad coughed, choking on his food, and everyone else was painfully quiet for what felt like an hour.

"Well . . ." I sighed. "That's awkward."

My dad snorted first. Then everyone else burst into hysterics.

"Wow." Sandi shook her head, wiping tears from her eyes. "This isn't usually how our dinner conversations go."

"Yes, it is," Luke said, giving her his devilish grin.

She laughed a surprisingly girly giggle. "OK, fine. That's exactly how it goes. What can I say? Welcome to our home."

I couldn't help smiling. Dad was right. Perfect would be boring, and the Waters family was anything but.

CHAPTER 20

5̃4 days left

When the sun had gone down, and it was time for my dad to go home, I walked him to the door. He paused and looked at me a few seconds too long, giving me that look he always had when we had to talk about something neither of us wanted to deal with.

"Nope," I said, cutting him off. "Don't want to talk about it."

Dad smiled and kissed me on the head. "OK, sweetie, we won't talk about it."

I looked over at the kitchen, where Luke and Megan were cleaning up the mess from dinner. "But I do need you to take something with you. Hang on, I'll be right back."

I ran back to Megan's room, where we had stashed the

pads Sandi had bought for me. I took out a handful for my stay and carried the bulky bag back to my dad.

"Can you take these with you?" I asked, refusing to look him in the eye.

"Sure, kiddo." He timidly took the bag from my hand. "Have fun tonight."

"OK."

"And, honey?"

"Yeah?" I looked up at him.

"I'm glad you've made some good friends." He looked at me like he had more to say. I could tell he was thinking about the past year—probably still wondering what happened.

"Me too." I opened the front door before he could say anything more.

Dad took the hint and looked over my head to wave goodbye to Sandi, who was standing in the distance behind us. "Thanks for everything," he said, awkwardly motioning with the pads in her direction.

"No problem." Sandi gave him that signature grin the whole Waters family seemed to possess.

Thirty minutes later, Megan and I were splayed out on the living room couch, surrounded by the junk food Sandi had bought us earlier. Sandi was cross-legged on the floor in front of us, queuing up the movie she wanted us to watch.

Just then Luke walked in. "What are y'all doing?" he asked, plopping down on the couch next to me and grabbing the box of chocolate-covered raisins from my lap.

"Just getting ready to watch my all-time favorite movie," Sandi said, hitting play. She whipped her head in our direction and said, "'Nobody puts Baby in the corner.'"

We all stared at her.

She waved us away. "You'll get it later after you watch the movie."

"What's it called?" Luke asked.

"*Dirty Dancing.*"

A few moments later, the opening credits came on, and a bunch of people were slow-motion dancing to an old song. They were all over each other, and I felt my face go red.

"Mom! This is inappropriate," Megan said.

Sandi scoffed. "No, it's not. It's fine. I watched it when it first came out, and I was your age. It's not that bad, I promise."

Megan and I looked at each other and giggled. Luke shifted uncomfortably next to me. I was waiting for him to get up, but he didn't. Eventually he settled in, grabbing the box of candy from my hand again.

"Luke, those are for Micah," Megan said.

"Why? Because she started her period?" He gave me that look—the one that I now knew meant he was trying to get under my skin. His eyebrow twitched every time he did it.

It worked every time.

"Luke!" Sandi yelled at him. "You and your brother, I swear. Micah is never going to come back here."

"What? Blame Megan. If it weren't for her, we wouldn't know anything!"

Megan darted a glare in his direction. "Oh yeah? Should we share with Micah what you and Daddy were talking about the other night?"

Luke's face turned pale, "Wh-what?" he stuttered.

"Enough, you two!" Sandi said, suddenly stern.

Megan was looking over at Luke with a smug look on her face, like she had just won some battle I couldn't see. I was dying to know what she was talking about.

"Have you ever tried these with popcorn?" Luke asked, trying to change the subject. He held the candy box up for me to see.

"No," I said, carefully eyeing him and Megan.

"Hang on," he said. "I'll be right back. Don't eat any more of those." He darted out of the room. A few minutes later he came back carrying a bowl of microwave popcorn. He grabbed the candy out of my lap and dumped the contents into the bowl.

"It's good, try it." He put the bowl between us and nestled in right next to me. I could feel his warm arm resting against mine and wondered if he was as aware of it as I was. Megan rolled her eyes.

As the movie progressed, I started to see why Sandi loved it so much. A nerdy girl named Baby went to a family summer camp type thing and met a handsome guy named Johnny who taught dance classes. His partner got sick or something, so Baby had to step in and take her place. Most of the movie was her learning how to dance with him.

At one point, Nick walked in to see what we were doing but stopped short when he saw what was on the TV. "Oh, hell no," he said and walked right back out.

I was trying to dig out the last of the raisins from the bottom of the bowl when Sandi turned around. "This is it! This is the scene I was talking about!" She turned back around to watch.

My hand was still in the popcorn bowl when I felt Luke's fingers wiggling around in the bowl too. We were fighting for the last bits of chocolate-covered raisins. I stopped looking for the candy and paid attention as Johnny walked right up to the table Baby was sitting at with her family. He stopped dramatically in front of them and said, "Nobody puts Baby in the corner."

I thought I would laugh at that moment, but I didn't. Right then I wanted to be Baby. I wanted someone to take my hand and lead me into a dance, just like Johnny did. I would never admit it, but I wanted that someone to be Luke.

Just then Luke's fingers shifted again in the popcorn,

and before I could take my hand out of the bowl, he linked his pinky to mine.

My face burned bright red. I couldn't bring myself to look at him. I was certain he could hear my heart bouncing off the walls of my rib cage. I glanced over at Megan to see if she knew what was happening. She was looking over at Luke and me and didn't look happy.

I didn't want to break that code she always talked about—especially not after she'd been so nice to me today—so I jerked my hand out of the bowl, unlinking my pinky from Luke's.

Disappointment seemed to radiate from his body, and I instantly wished I could take it back. I wanted to put my hand back in that popcorn bowl, but the moment had passed. The damage was done.

* * *

That night, as I lay in Megan's bed, I could hear her breathing softly next to me. I couldn't sleep. It wasn't because I was uncomfortable—in fact I was *really* comfortable. There was just something about the people in this house that made me feel good.

I hadn't had a friend like Megan in a long time. She was caring and supportive, the way a friend should be. But Luke had been my first friend in the neighborhood . . . maybe even more than that. I didn't know. I hated to think that I'd hurt his feelings tonight. After the movie had ended, he'd gone straight to his room without saying anything to us.

The truth was, if Megan hadn't been sitting there too, I would have let him hold my hand—or my pinky—forever. It felt good. It was a sign that maybe he liked me the way that I liked him.

Either that or he was just flirting with me like he did with everyone else. For all I knew, Luke held pinkies with all Megan's friends and that's why she was so against it.

One thing was for certain. It didn't matter what I did. I was going to end up making one of my friends mad at me, and I hated that. It was a feeling I knew all too well.

CHAPTER 21

53 days left

The next morning, I left Megan brushing her teeth and walked into the kitchen to find Sandi making more zucchini muffins. "Good morning . . . ," she sing-songed.

I smiled. "Good morning."

She reached for a bag sitting on the counter and handed it to me. "Here you go, sweetie. Put this by the door to take home with you later," she whispered.

When I peeked inside I saw my bathing suit. I quickly closed the bag again and blushed.

"Good as new." Sandi winked. "If it happens again, which it will, be sure to rinse it in cold water." She smiled, and I felt myself relax. Then she went back to grating zucchini as if the whole exchange had never happened.

Thirty minutes later, Megan and I were working on our second round of muffins when Luke stumbled into the kitchen. His dark hair jutted out in different directions as he sleepily made his way to the fridge and took a swig from the milk carton. I watched him, hoping for a sign he wasn't mad at me after what had happened the night before.

"Lukas Damarian!" Sandi shouted. "That is disgusting! Stop *doing* that!"

Luke waved his hand over his head as if he were trying to swat the nagging away from him. He didn't say a word, just stuck the carton back in the fridge and disappeared back into his room.

Just then I heard the front door open. "Megan!" Ava walked in without even knocking. "I'm back!" She was followed by Trish. "I've got gifts. My aunt took me to Venice Beach, and I got us all matching sunglass—"

Ava stopped short when she saw me sitting at the breakfast bar. Trish gave me her signature stink face.

"Oh . . ." Ava looked surprised, then smiled. "Hey, Micah."

"Do you girls want some muffins?" Sandi offered. She walked around the counter to greet Trish. "Haven't seen you in a while," she added, wrapping her arm around Trish's scrawny shoulder. "Where've you been?"

Trish gave her a half smile and shrugged into the hug. "I've just been at camp."

Megan looked over as if she were expecting Trish to say hello, but she never did. Instead, she kept scowling at me.

"Well, what do you guys want to do today?" Megan finally asked.

"I don't know." Trish shrugged.

Ava looked over at me and stuck the plastic bag she was carrying behind her back. "Whatever you guys want to do."

"Well, we've got to get ready," Megan said, pointing to me with her thumb, then looking down at the big T-shirts we'd slept in.

"Micah, I have spare toothbrushes in the linen closet if you want one," Sandi told me as she wiped down the counters.

"She needs one," Trish muttered.

I looked at her, and she gave a quick fake smile but let it drop just as quickly.

Oh joy.

Ava gave Trish a slight nudge with her elbow before they turned to follow Megan to her room. I was dreading going to Megan's room with Trish there, but I didn't see another option.

When I walked in, the room no longer felt inviting. Ava and Trish had plopped themselves down on the bed while Megan rummaged through her closet. I snuck past them and into the bathroom to find the linen closet with the toothbrushes in it.

"What. Is. *She* doing here?" I heard Trish stage whisper from the other room.

"She's hanging out with me," Megan replied. "What did you expect? You just . . . ditched me."

"I was at camp," Trish corrected.

"What about after camp?"

Trish didn't respond.

I found the pack of unused toothbrushes and grabbed the yellow one, running the bristles under the faucet and doing my best to ignore the conversation happening in the other room.

Just then the door to Luke's room opened. He made his way past me without even acknowledging me. He leaned against the doorframe to Megan's room and said, "Hey, Trish. Where've you been?"

"Did you miss me?" she asked, changing the tone of her voice completely.

"Who wouldn't?" Luke responded with a cocky grin.

I rolled my eyes. *Me!*

"How was California, Ava?" he asked.

"It was good!" she said sweetly.

Just by the sound of her voice I could tell that she was blushing. *About time she displayed normal behavior for a redhead.*

I couldn't find the toothpaste but spotted some deodorant and quickly swiped it on my armpits before Luke turned around. I got a whiff of it and realized it was *his* deodorant.

I tried to hurry and put the lid on and replace it before he noticed.

Luke turned away from Megan's room and made his way to his sink and started splashing his face. He still wouldn't look at me.

"Well," I heard Trish say from the other room, "if you want things to go back to normal get *rid* of her. She's weird."

I froze, staring down at my toothbrush, hoping Luke hadn't heard that. He reached over into my line of vision and squirted some toothpaste onto my toothbrush for me. Then he squirted some on his own and started brushing his teeth. I started brushing too, trying to drown out the conversation in the other room.

"Just give her a chance. She's actually really cool," I heard Megan say.

I finally braved a glance at Luke in the mirror. He gave me a quick wink, spit out his toothpaste, and wiped his mouth. Then he turned and faced me, watching me meticulously brush my teeth.

I was stalling so I didn't have to go back into Megan's room, and Luke just kept staring at me with that crooked grin. Finally he said, "You done? I have to pee."

"Oh!" I said, all flustered. "Sorry." I tried to spit out my toothpaste as daintily as possible, rinsed out my mouth, wiped my face, and scrambled back to Megan's room.

Luke shut the door behind me, locking me in my own personal hell.

"You should wear this," Megan said, throwing me a flowy yellow top with spaghetti straps that crossed at the back. "You can't wear a bra with it, though."

Trish snickered, then gave me an appraising look. "I've got an idea," she said, suddenly sounding sweet. "Let's give Micah a makeover."

"We always do makeup," Megan protested, sifting through her closet again. "Let's do something else for a change."

"Come on! It'll be fun," Ava chimed in. "Not all of us are as naturally beautiful as you are, Megan. Besides, my aunt taught me all kinds of new tricks while I was in California." She looked at me and smiled. "She's a makeup artist."

I nodded, not sure what to say to that. I couldn't tell if Ava was really being nice or if she was playing along with whatever Trish was plotting.

Ava turned back to the other girls. "We can even do her hair." She stood up next to me and fluffed my hair. "You have such pretty hair, Micah."

Megan shrugged, looking at me expectantly. "It's up to you."

I took a deep breath. Maybe this would win them over. Maybe if I did this they wouldn't think I was so weird anymore. Maybe then I'd fit in. I'd wanted a transformation before middle school. Maybe this was the moment I was waiting for—just like in the movies.

Nobody puts Baby in the corner.

"OK," I agreed.

Ava squealed with excitement and divvied us up— she would do Megan's makeup, and Trish would do mine. "Trish and I already have makeup on," she explained.

I resisted the urge to roll my eyes. Heaven forbid they go outside without it.

Trish positioned me away from the mirror so that I couldn't see. "It'll be a surprise," she said, cheerily.

Maybe she's not so bad after all, I thought.

Trish appeared to take her time and paid careful attention to what she was doing. I could feel her bubble-gum breath on my face as she ordered, "Close your eyes. . . . OK, now open them . . . close them . . . now blot. No, like this." She rubbed her lips together, making a smacking noise. Then she looked at me for a minute, smudged something down the bridge of my nose, and smiled.

I relaxed a little.

"Perfect." She gently tapped a brush on my nose and smiled. "Now turn, and we'll do your hair."

I couldn't wait to see what I looked like, but when I turned around, my heart sank. Trish had drawn big dramatic eyebrows—squared at the ends and way too close together—over my thin blond brows. My eyes were lined with thick black eyeliner and coated in different shades of green eye shadow that made them look squinty. There were brown shadows down the sides of my nose and along my cheekbones. I looked like the Wicked Witch of the West.

"So? What do you think?" Trish asked, looking expectantly at my reflection in the mirror.

Is she serious?

I couldn't tell if she was messing with me or really thought I looked good, so I forced myself to smile. I nodded my head like a doll with a broken neck, pleading with my eyes not to spring a leak.

"I have to pee," I blurted. Then bolted for the bathroom door.

"Wait, Micah! Let us see," Megan called after me.

I quickly closed the door, but when I turned, I realized Luke's door was wide open. I rushed to shut it, but as I did, Josh, Luke, and Ryan all looked up at me in unison. Their mouths dropped open in shock.

I slammed the door and locked it, then sat down on the toilet and cried as quietly as I could. What was I supposed to do? There was no escape.

"Did you see that?" I heard one of the boys ask. "What even *was* that?"

Someone chuckled. "I have no idea."

A moment later, there was a knock on Megan's door.

"What do you want now?" Megan asked. "Get out! There's not enough room for all of you."

All the boys must be in Megan's room, I realized. *This is my chance.*

I cracked open Luke's door and looked around. No one in sight. I bolted through his room and made my way to the hallway leading to the front door just in time to hear Luke ask, "What did you do to her?"

CHAPTER 22

53 days left

I cried all the way home. If the girls had thought I was weird before, they definitely thought so now.

Don't put Baby in the corner, I thought. *Pshh. Put Baby back in the corner, wayyy back in the corner.*

When I got to my house it was eerily quiet. Dad was at work, so all the lights were turned off, and the blinds were drawn. I washed my face, went into my room, and laid my head on my pillow. I could feel warm tears leaking out the sides of my closed eyes, trickling down my face and into my ears. The more the tears came, the more frustrated I felt.

Why am I even crying? Because someone put makeup on my face?

I didn't know for sure that Trish had tried to make me look bad. I didn't know anything about makeup. Maybe I just looked bad in it. Maybe I just had one of those faces.

After a while, I decided enough was enough. I wasn't just going to sit in my room and cry. It was doing nothing but making me feel more pathetic. I trudged into the living room and sat down on the couch, where I debated watching TV for about five minutes. Then I saw the photo albums sitting on the shelf.

I walked over and pulled down two of my favorite albums. The pictures were from when I was three or four years old, back when Mom had seemed the happiest. Back before I knew about her bad days . . . before I knew that her bad days meant Dad and I would have bad days too.

I scanned through the photos, looking at my chubby cheeks and the white-blond ringlets. I'd been so cute as a baby.

When did I get I all red-faced and awkward? I wondered as I turned the pages.

My eyes fell on a close-up of Mom and me together. We were sitting in the grass, her chest against my back, both of us facing the camera. I had my head thrown back in a laughing fit, and her arms were wrapped tightly around me. Mom's long, blond hair flowed behind her as she stared straight out through the plastic covering the photo, her big blue-green eyes looking right through me.

I looked at that photo for a long time, wishing I were beautiful like her. Everyone talked about how much Mom and I looked alike, but I didn't see it.

Suddenly it dawned on me—maybe *her* makeup would look good on me. Dad kept some of Mom's things in an old trunk. I'd seen it before, hidden away in the far reaches of his closet, but had only looked inside once. It was at the end of fourth grade, a few months after Mom had died. Bored and lonely, I'd stumbled upon it while I was snooping around the house to kill time.

Even then, the trunk had felt private. Dad had hidden it in his closet, clearly trying to conceal it from me. He'd never *said* I couldn't look in it, but it felt forbidden all the same. But that day, curiosity had gotten the better of me.

At first I'd been disappointed to see only clothes inside and had been about to close the lid when the warm, clean scent of her greeted me like magnolia blossoms on a warm summer day. The need to be near her had hit me, hard and sudden. The hollow feeling I had gotten used to just seemed to swallow me up, and without thinking, I'd climbed inside the chest and lay on top of her clothes, burying my face in what was left of my mother. I'd instantly felt drained, and before I knew it, I'd drifted off to sleep.

I didn't know how much time had passed, but I'd woken to my dad shouting at me from the doorway. "Micah! What were you thinking? Get out of there!"

He'd sounded panicked and angry, and at first, I'd thought he was mad at me for messing up my mom's clean clothes. I was covering her sweet scent with my musty, outdoor smell.

"I'm sorry," I'd whispered. I had tried to climb out of the trunk, swallowing back the tears that began to line my throat.

"No . . . honey, come here." Dad had held his arms out to me. "It's OK. You just scared me." His voice had hitched. "If that lid had closed on you, you could have suffocated. . . . I can't lose you too, kiddo."

He'd wrapped his arms around me that day and held me tight. I'd squeezed him back but couldn't help feeling guilty. He wasn't the one I wanted just then—the only person I wanted was my mom.

* * *

The throb of my swollen eyes brought me back to the here and now, where I sat with the photo albums still on my lap. I couldn't stop thinking about that trunk. It suddenly seemed so important. I had to find it.

I started in Dad's closet, where he'd hidden it at our old house, but it wasn't there. I tore through the rest of house, searching everywhere I could think of. I even looked in the shed in the backyard, but the trunk was nowhere to be found.

Maybe he got rid of it. My breath hitched. It was possible. We had moved to get away from Mom's death, after all.

Eventually, feeling defeated, I walked back to my room. As I walked down the hall, I glanced at the closet at the end of the hall. I hadn't looked there, but it was abnormally large for a linen closet.

A trunk could fit in there, I thought.

I opened the doors, took a deep breath, and started moving stuff around. At first all I could see were towels and sheets. But when I crouched down and pushed aside an old blanket, that's where I found it, safely hidden under the bottom shelf. I pulled the trunk toward me and hesitated before I unlatched the hooks, preparing myself to be greeted by the perfume that lingered inside. Instead, I was smacked with the rancid smell of mothballs.

Reaching inside, I pulled out some of the clothing that sat on top and uncovered a pair of old, red high-tops. I smiled. *Mom's lucky shoes.* At least that's what she'd always called them. She'd worn them to every one of my soccer games and insisted they were lucky whether we won or not.

I held one up to the bottom of my foot and was surprised to see that it would fit. Our feet would have finally been the same size.

I set the shoes aside and sifted through a pile of flowy dresses, digging deeper until my hands landed on a cloth bag—Mom's makeup bag.

Glancing at the full-length mirror on the door, I gingerly pulled the contents from the bag one by one: pink blush, shimmery brown-and-gold eye shadows, mascara, lipstick, powder in a brown circular case, a half-used bottle of concealer. I sat there in the hallway, staring in the mirror, and smudged the half-used concealer on my fingers, rubbing it into my face like lotion.

I looked weird and pale, like a shiny ghost.

I wiped the powder over the liquid on my face next, then used the blush brush to sweep some color on my cheeks. I stopped and stared at my reflection for a minute, watching my blond eyelashes blink back at me.

I decided to do my eyes too, hoping that would help. I wiped my fingertip on the glittery brown powder and lightly rubbed it on my eyelids. When I looked up, my eyes seemed green instead of blue. They did that sometimes when I cried, although my eyes were no longer red and swollen.

I untwisted the mascara next and wiped off some of the glop as I pulled it out. My eyes flinched every time I brought the wand close to my eyelashes. On the first pass, I got too close to my eyeball, making my eyes scrunch closed. When I opened them back up, it looked like I had two black eyes.

"Crap," I muttered and went into the bathroom to wash it off. Once my face was dry, I sat back down on the floor in the hall and tried again with a little more success. With every swipe of the wand my blond eyelashes began to appear, seemingly out of nowhere. It was like I had invisible eyelashes, and this magic wand made them appear one by one.

When I was done, I studied myself in the mirror. My eyes looked much bigger than usual. I stared into them for a long time, watching my pupils grow and shrink, looking for my mother's eyes. But they weren't there. All I could see was me.

I collected the makeup and put it back in the bag. I knew I should put it back in the trunk, so Dad wouldn't know I'd been snooping, but I couldn't let it go. Not just yet.

I'd just started piling the clothes back into the trunk to cover my tracks when a tiny scrap of paper caught my eye. It was a sketch of a bird on a branch, looking at me with its head cocked to the side as if asking a question. It looked just like the birds that gathered in the magnolia tree outside my window.

I knew immediately what it was—one of Mom's sketches. I dug deeper into the trunk and uncovered drawing after drawing, scribbled on all assortments of scrap paper. Neither Dad nor I brought up her drawings. They were just another item on the list of things we didn't talk about. But holding the scrap of paper between my fingers made it clear he had been collecting them too.

I was carefully putting the drawings back in the trunk

when I spotted the envelope. It wasn't sealed shut, just tucked closed and hidden in a far corner. Inside was a yellow piece of lined paper torn from a legal pad. The handwriting was written in cursive with black ink, but it was erratic and almost impossible to read. There were random drawings in the margins, so I knew it was Mom's. At the top, there appeared to be a grocery list of items of sorts, but below that was a letter addressed to my dad.

Dear Brent . . .

Looking down at the letter, my hand shook. I knew I should just fold it up and put it back. It wasn't meant for me. I was suddenly terrified that my dad was going to burst through the front door and catch me snooping through these things. I pictured his red-rimmed eyes from the time he'd caught me sleeping in the trunk, and it felt like I was being punched in the gut with guilt.

Deep down I already knew what the letter said, because deep down I knew what this was—her suicide note.

CHAPTER 23

53 days left

Curiosity got the better of me, and I read the note, even though I knew it was wrong. There were parts I couldn't read because the words were too rushed together, and some of it simply didn't make any sense. But my heart dropped at the words I could read.

She said she wasn't fit to be a mother or a wife, that the guilt of it all was too much. She'd never wanted this life or the pressures that came along with it. It was too much. *We* were too much. She was trapped. No matter what she did, she'd never be what we needed, and for that, she could never forgive herself. It was all too exhausting. She couldn't take it anymore.

I knew my mother had had her moments, but I didn't want to remember her like this. Reading her words, I was flooded with memories I had tried to block out. The times she had locked herself in her room and refused to get out of bed. The crying when she drank too much. The times she'd been silent and wanted the house to be silent too.

Toward the end, Dad and I had tiptoed around her and each other, trying to read her mood when she walked into a room. She was one extreme or another. Full of life and laughter . . . and then not. There was no in-between.

I tried to tell myself that she didn't mean it. That she'd loved us and was just having one of her moments. More than anything, I wanted to be able to forgive for her leaving me.

I carefully placed the letter back where I had found it. There was no way I could let my dad know I had read it. I wasn't even supposed to know that Mom had committed suicide. But I knew. I had always known.

* * *

I knew the night she died that there was something weird about the whole scene. It was mid-January, and I woke up in the middle of the night to a burning in my stomach. My face felt flushed. Something was wrong—I knew it immediately. I lay in bed, gripping a teddy bear whose fur was too itchy to actually snuggle.

I blinked in the dark as the gray dots of blurry vision swirled in front of me. They came together slowly, and through the specks, a woman's face emerged, hovering in the air above my bed. She looked familiar somehow.

I kept staring, trying to figure out if the woman was real or not. She smiled at me in a way that I knew was meant to comfort me, but it terrified me more than anything. I just wanted my mom, but I was too scared to move.

Finally I mustered up enough courage to slide out of my bed. I refused to look up at the woman as I bolted across the hall and into my parents' room. I went straight to my mom's side of the bed, like I always did when I had nightmares, but she wasn't there. Her side of the bed was empty.

I went to the other side and woke up my dad instead. I didn't even have time to tell him about the woman over my bed before he realized my mom was gone. He looked terrified, like he knew something I didn't, and immediately flung off his covers. The next thing I knew, I was struggling to keep up with him as he rushed through the house.

As we made our way toward the kitchen, I could hear a rumbling coming from the garage. It sounded like the car was running.

Mom? Where is she going in the middle of the night?

I followed my dad into the kitchen, and as soon as he opened the door to the garage, the house was flooded with fumes. My stomach churned at the overwhelming smell of exhaust.

Dad slammed his hand frantically on the garage door

opener, causing the door to groan open, then closed, then open again. As he raced into the garage, he shouted back at me, "Stay inside, Micah! Get my phone, and call 911!"

I stood there, frozen. I couldn't move. I just watched as he yanked open the car door and pulled Mom's limp body from the car. She looked like she was in a deep sleep, and her nightgown rode up as he pulled her out.

Dad turned and saw me still standing there. "Micah!" he screamed. "Go!"

I ran back inside and did what he asked. I don't even remember picking up the phone, let alone what I said to the dispatcher. All I remember is sitting in the living room, staring blindly through the glass door, watching Dad trip over himself as he dragged Mom to the grass. Her nightgown was still pulled up too high, and her underwear was showing. I wanted to go out there and cover her up, but I was too scared.

Eventually I gathered enough courage to stand at the glass door. I hovered in the doorway, letting the cold air hit my wet cheeks.

Dad finally managed to get Mom to the grass under the old oak tree and shook her shoulders. When she didn't respond, he started screaming. "Sara! Look at me! Wake up, Sara!" He gathered her in his arms and rocked her back and forth. "How could you do this to yourself?" he cried. "Don't leave me . . . please don't leave!"

I froze in the doorway, and the air left my lungs. *Mom did this on purpose?*

Eventually a few people came out into their yards. Others hid in their houses and looked out the windows. The ambulance finally arrived, and the tree limbs that hung above my mother suddenly came to life, flickering in blue and red. The lights cast shadows across her face and body, giving the illusion that she was moving.

The next thing I knew our neighbor, Mrs. Sanders, came into our living room and led me out through my backyard so I couldn't see what the paramedics were doing. I took one last glance behind me, memorizing the sight of the tree flickering over the top of the house before I was forced to walk away.

Mrs. Sanders took me to her house and ushered me into her bedroom, where I was expected to sit on her flower-print bed and wait. She turned the TV on and went back outside.

I don't know how long I sat there, but suddenly I felt sick and ran to the bathroom to throw up. When I came back, I turned off the TV and sat in the dark. I wasn't sure if it was my imagination, but I could still see the blue and red flickering in the darkness.

It felt like forever before my dad appeared in the doorway. His eyes were swollen and red, and he held a rag up to his mouth as if trying to hold back the words he had come to say.

I wanted to help, so I said it for him. "Daddy, she's gone."

He nodded, fell to his knees, and sobbed. That's when I finally cried—great big gulping sobs, like I was gasping for air I could never get enough of. I was drowning. We both were.

I don't remember how we got home. I just remember lying on my mom's side of the bed, my dad next to me, and both of us crying until my head pounded and my ears rang.

By the end of the week, I was sitting at the funeral. It still didn't feel real. None of it did. I stared at the wax figure in the casket that was supposed to be my mom. I watched as tears ran down my aunt's cheeks, and I tried to urge my eyes to water too. But I couldn't. I just couldn't wrap my mind around it. The pain was too much.

I'm a horrible daughter, I thought. *I can't even cry at my own mom's funeral.*

After the funeral, everyone came back to our house, where people huddled together in small groups, talking in whispers. I overheard some of my mom's friends in the kitchen as I made my way to the backyard. Libby's mom, Kristen, was among them. I had hoped Libby would be with her, but she was spending winter break with her dad in San Antonio.

"I just saw her," one of my mom's friends sobbed. "She was fine. I just don't know what made her do this."

When they saw me, they all stopped talking and looked

at me with pity—it was a look I'd seen a lot of in the past week, and I was quickly growing to hate it. I slipped past them and went outside to find my cousins arguing in the backyard.

Jenny and Adam were a couple years older than I was and lived eight hours away in South Texas. Normally I would have been super-excited to see them. But that day, as I sat there listening to them bicker, all I wanted was for them to go away.

"It's true! That's how she died," Adam was saying.

"No. She died of carbon monoxide," Jenny said in her know-it-all voice.

"Yeah, that's how she committed suicide."

"What?" I asked. I hated that they were talking behind my back, like I wasn't there.

They both turned around to face me. "Nothing," Adam said. But I could tell he was trying to hide it from me, just like everyone else.

I couldn't stand it anymore. Did people really think I couldn't hear what they were saying? That I wasn't smart enough to figure it out?

Later, after everyone had left, I found my dad standing outside in the front yard by himself. He was sneaking a cigarette and stubbed it out when he saw me walk up.

"Hey, kiddo." He tried to smile through his tears. I'd never seen him look so haggard.

I had come on a mission. I was going to tell him what I knew. He clearly knew the truth. Everyone did. So why were they trying to keep me in the dark?

But as I stood there looking at him, I didn't know how to begin. My resolve started to fade.

"Dad?" My voice was barely a whisper.

At first he didn't seem hear me. He just stood there, staring at the tree where we had last seen Mom. Finally he turned toward me, but there was something about the look on his face that made me hesitate.

But I have to tell him . . . right?

I forced the words out, different than I'd intended. "How did Mom die?" I wanted to hear the truth from him.

Dad froze, and his chin began to quiver. Tears pooled in his eyes, and he stared everywhere but at me. It made me wish I had never asked.

"It was . . . carbon monoxide . . . from the car," he finally said. I waited for him to say the rest, but he wouldn't look at me. "It was an accident."

I looked away from him, disappointed, but I nodded like I believed him anyway. I suddenly realized why no one would tell me—they were trying to protect me. But a lie was a lie.

When I looked back up, Dad was looking right at me. Pleading with his eyes for me to believe him, to not ask any questions he couldn't answer.

And so I didn't. The only way I could offer him any relief was to lie to him too, and I'd do anything to ease his pain. I walked away, promising myself I would never ask him about it again. He could never know what I knew. I never wanted to see that look on his face again.

CHAPTER 24

53 days left

I put Mom's trunk back where it belonged and laid low for the rest of the day. Clouds had rolled in, and I could hear thunder rumbling outside, the perfect weather for hiding away from the world.

Before long, it started to pour. I thought I heard someone knocking on the door through the sound of the heavy rain, but I ignored it, feeling too drained to talk to anyone. Instead, I snuggled under the covers in my bed and got lost in a book while the storm rumbled on.

I must have lost track of the time because it was a surprise when Dad popped his head through the door. "Hey, kiddo. Whatcha doing?"

I jerked my head up. I hadn't heard him come in over

the sound of the storm. "Just reading," I said, putting down my book.

"How did last night go?" he asked.

"What?"

"The sleepover. How'd it go?"

"Oh, it was fun, I guess." He stood at the door waiting for more. "We just watched a movie and ate junk food," I said. "Then a few of Megan's friends came over this morning and decided to do a makeover."

Dad raised his eyebrows to that. "Oh really?"

"Yeah."

"And how'd that go?"

"I cried."

"Oh," he said, surprised. "You don't look bad. Are you wearing makeup now?"

"Yeah." I suddenly wished I hadn't brought it up. "I washed off the stuff Trish did."

"Well, where'd you get that stuff then?" Dad asked, gesturing to my face.

"Um . . ." I hesitated, trying to decide if I should lie or not. I didn't want him to know what I had found in the trunk, but before I could come up with an answer Dad's eyes flickered toward my mom's makeup bag on my dresser, then to the red high-tops sitting on my bed.

"You found her stuff," he said.

"Yeah."

Dad paused, and I could tell he was trying to steady his face. "Well, it looks nice on you," he finally said. He gave a weak smile, then walked over to my bed and kissed me on the cheek.

* * *

That night, after Dad was asleep, I snuck back to the trunk in the hallway to put mom's makeup back where it belonged. I had changed my mind about wanting to wear it. When I went to replace it, I noticed that the envelope was gone.

CHAPTER 25

51 days left

I woke up to the sun streaming in through my curtains and glanced at the clock on my nightstand. It was already mid-morning. My heart sank a little, realizing that Luke must not have come by.

Don't be stupid, I told myself. *It's not like he promised to show up every day.*

I just always hoped that he would.

I lay back in bed, blinking up at the ceiling, when a very familiar smell wafted into my room: pancakes and bacon, our old Saturday breakfast tradition. I loved those mornings because Dad would always let me help, even if it meant that there would be eggshell in our breakfast.

I slid out of bed and walked into the kitchen, still rubbing the sleep out of my eyes when I stopped short. Dad was sitting at the kitchen table, but he wasn't alone. Three familiar boys sat across from him. They all turned to face me at the same time.

"About time you woke up," Josh said, grabbing the last piece of bacon.

Ryan started to get up from his chair. "Here, you can have my seat."

Dad put a hand on Ryan's shoulder. "That's OK, buddy. I'll get up." He turned to me.

"We saved some pancakes for you. Do you want me to cook you up some eggs too?"

Josh's face turned green, and Luke, Ryan, and I all laughed.

"What?" Dad asked.

"Nothing." I giggled. "Eggs would be great." I eyeballed Josh as I took the seat next to him. "Make sure the yolk is *super*-runny."

Josh stifled a gagging noise, and I laughed. *That'll teach him to eat all my bacon.*

"OK . . ." My dad gave me a strange look.

When Dad's head was in the fridge, I turned to Luke. "What are you doing here?" I whispered.

"What do you mean? I come here every day."

"Yeah, but not here." I gestured to the table covered in dirty dishes.

Ryan leaned forward. "Your dad was outside watering

the yard and caught us standing outside your window." He looked at Luke accusingly. "It was super-embarrassing."

"Yeah, man, that's creepy stuff," Josh said, looking at him too. "You've been hanging out with Garrett too much."

"Oh! That reminds me, Dean and Garrett are meeting us at my house," Luke said, changing the subject. "We'd better hurry."

"So, how's soccer training going?" my dad asked from the other side of the kitchen.

"Great!" Luke said. "We have about a month until tryouts, so plenty of time. But Micah's got nothing to worry about. She could make the team with her eyes closed. Oh, before I forget, my mom wanted to know if y'all had plans for the Fourth."

Dad cracked an egg into the pan. "The Fourth? Wow, that's coming up. Monday, right?"

"Yup," Luke said. "We always cook out at our house and then head over to the carnival. Mom said if you're interested you should stop by."

My dad turned to me and smiled. "What do you think, Micah? Should we go?"

I shrugged. "Sure."

I wondered if Trish would be there too. *Ugh, probably.* There was no way she'd miss out on her plans to kiss Luke.

* * *

After breakfast, we got ready to head to Luke's house for practice. On the porch, I reached for my skateboard out of habit, but Luke stopped me. "Actually we had to walk here," he said.

"Why?" I asked.

"My stupid brother ran over my board with his car." Josh sulked.

That's when I noticed the plastic bag containing my clean bathing suit sitting next to my board. I'd totally forgotten it in my hurry to get out of the Waters's house the day before.

Luke saw me looking at it and picked it up. "Megan came by to give this to you yesterday, but she said you weren't home. I think she was worried about you."

So I *had* heard someone knocking yesterday. I was touched, but also embarrassed. I snagged the bag from Luke and clutched it to my chest.

"What's in it?" Josh asked.

My face turned red. "Nothing," I said, opening the front door and throwing the bag into the house without looking. It made a crinkly sound as it hit my dad in the face.

"What the—" The door shut, cutting him off.

Josh and Ryan looked at me like I was a weirdo, and Luke snickered. I looked at him and glared. *Don't you dare tell them.*

"Why was Megan worried about you?" Ryan asked.

"Yeah . . . what was that all about anyway?" Luke asked. "You looked really weird yesterday. Did Trish do that to you?"

"Yeah." I walked off the porch, leaving the boys behind me. I didn't know what was more suffocating, this conversation or the humidity. The rain from the day before hung in the air, making my shirt cling to my back.

"What was she trying to do to you?" Josh asked as they all hurried down the walkway to catch up with me.

"It was supposed to be a makeover," I admitted, slowing down a bit.

"It didn't work." Josh laughed. "You looked like a zombie swamp monster thing. Was that supposed to look good?"

I laughed too. "I have no idea." For some reason it was a relief to know that I wasn't the only one who'd thought it was hideous.

"Why would you want a makeover anyway?" Luke asked.

I shrugged.

"Don't let them turn you into one of them," he said, setting the pace as we walked down the sidewalk toward his house.

"What? A hottie?" Josh asked. "Why not?"

Luke turned to me. "I like you the way you are." I felt my heart inflate. "You're one of us."

My heart sank. *Right . . . I'm just one of the boys.*

"Yeah, man. You're like a straight up *haus,*" Josh said. "Look at your legs, they're bigger than mine." He lifted his shorts to show his pasty white thighs.

I looked down at my own legs and realized he was right.

"I wish I had muscles like that," Ryan chimed in.

"Seriously, dude. Do you do squats or something?" Josh asked.

"No." Then I thought about it. "Well, *now* I do."

"Let's hurry up and get to your house," Josh said to Luke. "I need to make some gains if I'm going to be half the man Micah is."

Seriously? I must have been scowling, because Josh reached up to grab the tree limb hanging over my head and gave it a good shake. The rain from the night before drenched me.

"Hey!" I squealed. "Why'd you do that?"

"You looked like you needed to cool down a little." Josh laughed.

I grabbed the limb above him in retaliation and gave it a tug, soaking all of us. We all laughed and took turns grabbing tree limbs from yard to yard as we walked to Luke's house. By the time we arrived, we were soaked through. We went straight to the backyard, where we heard Dean and Garrett talking behind the fence.

"Do you think the girls are inside?" Garrett was asking as we made our way through the side gate.

"Who cares?" Luke said, leading Dean and Garrett into the shed to dig out the training equipment. He returned carrying a stack of orange cones. "We're more fun than they are, anyway." He grinned. "Trust me."

Despite what he'd said, I glanced toward the back of the house. I also wondered if the girls were inside. I didn't even want to know what they thought of me after I ran off the day before.

After Luke set down the last cone, he stood up straight and brushed off his hands. "All right, let's do some timed sprints to see who's the fastest," he said, setting us to work.

After I beat all the boys—twice—we did burpees, which I really sucked at, sled pulls using an actual sled weighed down by Keaton, and enough lunges and squats to make a person want to cry.

Afterward, I found myself lying in the grass, drowning in my own sweat, legs wobbly and lungs burning. I looked over at the boys all gathered around the side of the house, drinking from the water hose, and felt a twinge of jealousy. They'd all stripped off their shirts after the first sprint, and here I was, suffocating in my T-shirt.

Just then Sandi popped her head through the back door. "Luke! Stop drinking from the water hose. It's not safe!"

"Who says?" Luke asked.

"I say!" she yelled back.

Sandi disappeared back inside, but the door didn't stay closed for long. A moment later, Megan came out, followed by Ava and then Trish.

"Closed practice, ladies," Luke said. He sprayed the hose in their direction to shoo them away, and Trish let out her flirty squeal.

Megan rolled her eyes. "We're not here to see *you*. We're here to see Micah."

"Yeah, well, she earned her way here," Luke said. "Go jump off a high dive or something, and then you can come back."

Megan ignored her brother and made her way toward me, motioning for Trish and Ava to join her. Trish ignored her, making a beeline for Luke and the boys instead. Creepy Garrett's face lit up.

"Hey," Megan said as she walked over. "I came over yesterday . . ." She trailed off, looking a little hurt, and I couldn't meet her eyes. "I wanted to make sure you were OK."

I could tell that she was looking for answers, but I didn't know what to say. I didn't know how to explain what had happened.

"Well, you're looking good out here," Megan said after a moment of silence, letting me off the hook. "You're definitely going to make the team if you keep this up."

I looked down, feeling even more guilty. I had no real

intention of trying out. I'd told Luke that from the beginning, but based on his comments this morning, he clearly thought I'd changed my mind. I didn't want to correct him, not if it meant giving up my excuse to hang out with him— with all of them.

Ava sat down in the chair next to Megan. "You're going to love our team!" she gushed. "We play in a league in Dallas and go on lots of overnight trips—"

"And flirt with boys in the hotels," Trish chimed in from across the yard. She looked straight at Luke when she said it.

Luke stiffened, then took another swig of water from the hose. I tried not to notice how jealous he got at the idea of Trish flirting with other boys.

"Gosh, Ryan, stare much?" Trish laughed suddenly.

I looked over to see Ryan looking at me. His ears turned bright red, and he looked down, pretending to study the grass beneath him.

"Seriously you two," Trish said, looking at me now, "when are you going to just admit that you like each other and get it over with?" She linked her arm through Luke's and gestured to them both. "I mean, *we* get it. Not everyone is as mature about dating as Luke and I are, but seriously, Ryan, just ask Micah to watch the fireworks with you already!"

Ryan's eyes met mine, then dropped again.

"It's official then," Trish said with finality. She looked at me with that fake smile and squealed. "Now we've *both* got dates!"

Dates? What is she even talking about? We're twelve.

I looked over at Ryan. He looked like I felt—like he wanted to crawl into a hole and die.

CHAPTER 26

51 days left

I stood in the shower, shivering under the cool water as it pelted my skin. My face was still burning with embarrassment, for both me *and* Ryan. Shortly after Trish's declaration, Ryan had made an excuse to leave, clearly embarrassed. Everyone else had decided to go swimming, but since I was now a part of the Being-a-Girl-Sucks Club, swimming wasn't an option at the moment.

Ugh. When will this end?

I put on a light-pink tank top, one of my newer shirts, with a pair of jean shorts, and was brushing my hair as I walked into the kitchen to get a drink. Dad was sitting at the table with his laptop, probably doing some sort of nerdy geologist stuff for work, even though it was the weekend.

"Hey, kiddo," he said without looking up. "How'd training go?"

"It was good."

We were both quiet for a moment, with only the sound of him typing and me brushing. Finally I asked, "Dad?"

"Hmm?" he replied as he continued to type.

"What's a *haus*?"

Dad stopped typing. "Why?"

"Because the boys were talking about how I had huge legs, and Josh called me a *haus*. Is that bad?"

"I don't think so, honey. I think it was probably supposed to be a compliment. You know, like how you call somebody a beast if they're super-athletic?"

I wrinkled my nose. That didn't sound any better.

Dad went back to typing, but when I continued to stand behind him he stopped and sighed. "OK, fine. Let's Google *haus* and see what the definition is. That will tell us whether or not it's a good thing."

The first thing that popped up were German restaurants—apparently *haus* meant building or house in German.

"Great!" I wailed. "I'm as big as a house."

"Wait just a minute. You don't know that's what he meant. Do any of those boys speak German?"

"I don't think so," I admitted.

"So we can probably rule out that definition." Dad

scrolled some more. "Wait a minute. What is this?" He clicked on the Urban Dictionary definition for *haus*:

haus

A term given to a person who is amazing in all aspects of life.

To be really, really ridiculously good at something

Dad leaned back in his chair. "Well, there you have it," he said, grinning at me like one of the boys. "You must be really, *really* ridiculously good at soccer."

"They were talking about how huge my legs were," I said, standing up to show him.

"Honey, that's called muscle. And let me tell you," he said, dead serious, "there is nothing more attractive than a strong woman."

I cringed at the word *woman*—I was *not* ready to think of myself like that—but couldn't help smiling a bit.

"I think it's great that you're playing soccer again," Dad continued. He beamed at me proudly. "I looked into the team, and it seems like a great fit. It's a little expensive, but we can make it happen. It's worth it to see you play again, to see you getting back to yourself."

I didn't know what to say to that. He seemed so happy about the possibility. . . . I didn't know how to tell him I wasn't planning on trying out.

"You know . . . ," he said tentatively. "I've been thinking about yesterday."

I looked up at him. *Oh no. He knows I saw the letter.*

"I don't think it's a good idea for you to be wearing your mom's makeup."

I stiffened, feeling guilty about using the makeup, guilty about finding the note, guilty for reading it.

"That stuff has probably gone bad by now anyway. And . . ." He hesitated. "Well . . . I was thinking maybe we could see if we can get one of those makeup-counter ladies to help. You know, teach you how to wear makeup. If that's what you want." He hurried to add. "Then maybe you can get some of your own. What do you think?"

I felt myself relax a little. We weren't going to talk about the letter. Maybe he didn't know.

"OK." I agreed. I'd even let Trish do my makeup again if that meant we didn't have to talk about what I'd found in the trunk.

CHAPTER 27

51 days left

Fifteen minutes later, we were sitting in my dad's truck with the windows rolled down because the A/C wasn't working. My face was red and sweaty again as I looked at my reflection in the side mirror. Music was blasting from the speakers, and my dad was singing along with the radio in his loud, off-key voice. I could have sworn people were staring at us as we pulled into the mall parking lot.

"*She's a brick . . . house. . . . She mighty-mightay . . . ,*" Dad belted out as he parked.

I rolled my eyes—Dad was seriously the worst singer I'd ever heard in my life—but I couldn't help laughing out loud and joining in.

By the time we walked through the air-conditioned doorway leading into the mall, my hair was sticking to my sweaty neck, so I ditched the braid and swept my hair up into a messy bun. Dad and I walked through the makeup stations in silence. Clearly neither of us had any idea where to go, so we just browsed around, sniffing perfumes and hoping someone would walk up and offer to help.

"Here, smell this one," I said, sticking a lotion under his nose. It smelled like lemon and vanilla. I squeezed the bottle a little, trying to make the air gently waft the scent toward his face. Instead, a big glob of lotion smacked him right under the eye.

"Hey!" Dad shouted, wiping it off. "Smell this!" He picked up a random bottle and sprayed it in my direction.

"Can I help you?" I heard someone ask behind me. I turned and saw a woman wearing what looked to be a lab coat and tons of makeup.

"Oh umm . . ." My dad tried to gently put the bottle back down on the glass counter, but it toppled over, making a loud, clattering noise. "We're here to see if someone could help my daughter learn how to do her . . ." He drew air circles around his face, like he had suddenly become a mime.

"Her makeup?" the woman asked, looking amused.

"Yeah, her makeup."

"Of course, follow me." She turned on her heel and started walking away.

I turned to my dad and made circular motions around

my face. We both started laughing and couldn't stop. I ended up snorting, and my dad had already started his wheeze laughing. There was no stopping once that got started. By the time we made it to where the saleslady was waiting, I had tears streaming down my face.

The saleslady led me to the makeup counter and plopped me down in a chair. I spent the next thirty minutes opening my eyes, shutting my eyes, and blotting my lips. She told me what she was doing every step of the way, while Dad hovered over her shoulder like a weirdo—apparently taking notes.

"Wait," he interrupted at one point. "Does she put eyeliner on *before* or after she does the mascara?"

At least he's paying attention.

I told the saleslady I wanted a more natural look, so she picked neutral colors, but I was still afraid to look in the mirror when she was finished. I kept thinking about the green eye shadow from my last makeover and how it had made my eyes look all squinty and snarly.

In the end, it still looked a little caked on, but it was much better than what Trish had done to me.

The woman looked a bit disappointed when I only ended up with a palette of glittery eye shadow made of browns and creams, powder, mascara, and a light pink lip gloss. "Are you sure you wouldn't like some eyeliner to go with that?" she asked.

"No, we're good," my dad assured her, handing over his credit card. "We've got other things to purchase."

I looked at him. "We do?"

"Yep." He handed me the bag of makeup as we walked away from the counter.

"What do we have to buy?"

"Umm, well . . . I think we need to get you some . . ." Dad looked straight ahead, not making eye contact with me, and gestured to his chest. "Some bras or something."

I stared at him with my mouth gaping open. I had never really envisioned this moment—the one where I went bra shopping for the first time—but if I had, this was *not* how I would have wanted it to go.

"No way," I said, suddenly finding my voice. "I'm not bra shopping with you!"

"I agree," Dad said, looking relieved. "Here, take this." He shoved his credit card in my direction as if it might suddenly grow teeth and bite him.

"What? You can't just leave me."

"Sure I can. Just walk over there where that . . . stuff is." He gestured to where the sexy pajamas were, then hesitated when he spotted a mannequin wearing lingerie. "But . . . don't buy that."

"Ew! *Dad!* What do I do?"

"I don't know! Does it look like I have . . . breasts?"

"Dad!" I yelled again. He was losing it.

"Just try stuff on until you find one that fits." His face was just as red as mine felt. "I'm going anywhere but here. I'll be right outside the store . . . sitting on a bench or something."

With that, he touseled my hair, making my bun lopsided, and walked off as quickly as he could. He looked from side to side, as if trying to make sure no one saw him, as he walked away in clipped steps.

What a nerd. No wonder I'm so awkward.

I wandered into the lingerie department with no idea where to begin. I looked at the different sizes, but all I knew was that the farther down the alphabet, the bigger the boob.

I was holding a bra up to my chest when a kind older lady approached me. "Has anyone helped you yet, sugar?" she asked.

"Uh, no," I said, trying to return the smile.

"What size are you normally?"

"Um . . . I don't know."

"Oh!" The woman suddenly seemed to realize this was my first visit. She glanced around as if looking for someone—probably the adult I was supposed to be shopping with, the one guiding me through this pivotal moment in my life.

"My dad's . . . in the men's department," I lied. I didn't want to have to explain to her that he'd just ditched me.

"*Oh,*" she said in an even kinder voice. "Well, let's see

what we can do here. I have a pretty keen eye, but I think it would be best if we measured you."

I felt a hot wave of panic wash over my body. *Uh-oh . . . am I going to have to take my shirt off in front of this lady?*

She took me to the dressing room and handed me a different top—tighter than the one I was wearing—to change into. My body eased with relief.

At least I don't have to get naked in front of her.

Once I was changed, she ran the measuring tape around my rib cage, under my boobs, and then once again over my boobs. "Well, dear, it looks like you're a thirty-two B. That's what I thought."

"I'm a B?"

She gave me another kind smile. "Yes, ma'am. It looks like you've been needing a bra for some time. Unless you grew overnight, which does seem to happen sometimes." She gave me another knowing smile. I couldn't help but grin back.

This lady is like a boobie expert.

"Now, let's see what we can find you. . . ."

I changed back into my shirt and followed the saleslady through the racks as she randomly picked out different bras.

"You'll want a nude-colored bra to go under white shirts," she said, handing one to me. "And if you like to wear tank tops, you might want to buy a racer back."

"What's that?" I asked.

"Oh, it's just a bra where the straps are attached in the middle of your back. That way they don't show on your shoulders. The bra usually opens in the front."

Huh?

"Here you go, sugar." She pointed to the rack. "There are all types of colors, so you can choose whatever you want."

"Will they show through my shirt?"

"Sometimes you can't help but see the straps, depending on the sleeves. Some girls choose bright colors that coordinate with their clothes, so it just looks like it's a part of the ensemble. Oh, and they have bandeaus, which are meant to be seen. Say you're wearing a tank top, but it's a bit looser under your arms—just put on one of these, and it'll complement your outfit and provide coverage. It doesn't really provide much support, though. Some girls wear them with sundresses as well. We have some over here somewhere. . . ."

She started wandering off. Just then I saw my dad in the aisle, looking uncomfortable again. He was still standing a bit away, but once he saw me with the saleslady he looked relieved. He gave me a thumbs-up and raised his eyebrows as if to say, *You good?*

I nodded and smiled. *This lady is awesome.*

"Here they are," she said, returning with a handful of bras on hangers. "What else? Do you play sports? You must with a figure like that."

I looked at myself in one of the mirrors. *What does that mean?*

"If I had legs like that, I would be strutting around in high heels all the time just showing 'em off." She sighed. "Oh, to be young again."

I smiled at her and looked in the mirror again. My arms and legs did look lean and muscular. I stood a bit taller.

"If you play sports, you'll want a sports bra," the woman continued. "We have some over here."

After trying on all the items, I decided to buy two sports bras, one regular nude-colored bra, a pink racer back, and a lacy white bandeau with watermelon slices on it. It came out to be quite a lot, but I figured my dad deserved it for abandoning me.

CHAPTER 28

49 days left

I could feel the heat radiating through my window, even though the day had just begun. It seemed to be getting hotter and hotter every day. I was about to roll out of bed when I realized what day it was—the Fourth of July.

I pulled the covers over my head and groaned. I'd been dreading this day. I couldn't stop picturing the way Trish had her arm linked through Luke's the other day—that and the smug look she'd had on her face when she pretty much announced they were dating.

Are they dating? When did that even happen?

I just lay there, breathing in the stale air from under my covers, when I heard knocking on my door.

"Go away, Dad!" I yelled through my comforter. "I'm sleeping!"

I heard the door slowly unlatch, and I didn't have to uncover my face to know that Dad was lurking in the doorway. I waited for him to say something, but he remained silent. I was just about to uncover my face when I felt something heavy pounce on me.

"Wakey, wakey!"

That is not *my dad.* I uncovered my head. "Luke? What are you doing here?"

"You were supposed to be at my house, like"—he looked at his phone—"thirty minutes ago."

"It's a holiday," I argued, trying to cover my face again to hide my morning breath.

Luke grabbed the blankets before I could and gave me a devious grin. "No rest for the wicked! Get dressed."

"I'm not going."

"Why not?" He looked down at me with his eyebrows etched together. "Is it because your boyfriend is there?" he taunted.

And what about your girlfriend? I wanted to yell at him. *Will she be there?*

Instead I said, "He's not my boyfriend! I don't even like Ryan!" It came out harsher than I'd intended.

Luke looked down at me for a minute like he was trying to decide whether I was telling the truth or not.

"Not like that anyway," I finished, a bit calmer.

Luke studied me for a minute longer, his expression unreadable, then said, "It doesn't matter anyway. Ryan won't be there. After you both rushed off yesterday I told everyone we weren't training today."

"What? Then why are you making me get up?"

Luke didn't say anything.

I sat up in my bed. "Why do you even care?"

He stood up and shrugged, ignoring my question. "Get your lazy butt up. I'll wait for you in the living room."

I took my time getting ready. If Luke was going to be pushy, he could wait. By the time I walked into the living room, he had made himself at home in front of the TV.

"Where's my dad?" I asked, looking around. There was no sign of him.

"He's mowing the lawn," Luke said, turning off the TV. "Come on, let's go to my house. Your fridge is, like, empty."

We walked out the front door, and I went to grab my skateboard—Ryan's skateboard—but thought better of it at the last minute. Instead I walked around to the already open garage door. I stuck the longboard inside and grabbed my neglected bike. I nearly ran Luke over as I made my way out of the garage.

"Hey!" He laughed. "You look like a dork on that thing!" he yelled after me as I rode away.

"So?" I shouted back, riding off without him in the direction of his house.

A few moments later, I heard Luke's skateboard rolling up behind me. We didn't talk, but every now and then I would catch him shooting me a sideways glance.

"Stop doing that," I finally said as we rounded the corner to his block.

"What?"

"Looking at me like Garrett. It's creepy."

Luke laughed. "He does have sort of creepy eyes, doesn't he?"

I couldn't help but laugh back. "Totally."

When we got to his house, Luke rode his board right to the front door and waited for me. I kicked at the rusty kickstand of my bike about a thousand times before it finally gave way.

"How old were you when you got that thing?" Luke asked when I finally made my way toward him.

"Eight, but it was a hand-me-down," I said as we went inside. I expected to be greeted by the usual chaos of the Waters's house, but it was strangely silent. "Where is everyone?"

"Keaton went fishing with my dad, and my mom is around here somewhere."

"Where's Megan?" I asked. Things still felt a little weird between us after the makeover fiasco. Even if she had seemed mostly normal the other day, I could tell she was a little bothered by the way I had run off. A part of me wanted to talk to her about it, explain what had happened, but a bigger part of me just wanted to hide.

"She spent the night at Ava's house with Trish. I think they've got some weird master plan for the fireworks tonight." Luke wiggled his eyebrows.

I just glared at him.

"Don't you want to know what they have planned?" he asked.

"Nope." I kept it short, instead of saying what was really going through my head: *No, I don't want to know, you idiot! I don't want to know how Trish plans on kissing you while the fireworks blaze in the sky. I'm just fine not knowing that, thank you very much!*

"Why are you looking at me like that?" Luke asked as he made his way toward the refrigerator.

"Like what?"

"Like you're shooting laser beams at me with your eyeballs."

I tried to relax my face. "I'm not."

"Yes, you are." He smirked and cracked two eggs into the pan. "Look, I'm not the one who set you up on a date tonight."

"You know that's stupid, right? I'm twelve. I don't go on dates."

"Maybe not, but you can still watch the fireworks on the soccer field where all the other twelve-year-olds go when they like someone enough to kiss them."

I just looked at him while he poured a glass of orange juice and handed it to me. I didn't want to know how he knew that.

"Anyway, you'd better watch out," he said. "Trish and Ava have big plans for you tonight."

"How do you know?"

Luke held up an iPad with a pink case on it. "It's Megan's. And it's synced to her phone," he said with a devilish grin. He set the iPad back down and buttered two pieces of toast. "I've been spying on her with this forever. You're lucky I can't use it on you too." He winked.

"Why would you want to spy on me? I'm with you all the time. You already know everything."

"Not everything," he said. "I don't know who you like."

"I don't like anyone!" I snapped.

"You're lying. I can tell." Luke slid the eggs onto a plate, plopped the toast on top, and handed it to me. "Two eggs over easy and two pieces of toast with tons of butter. Just the way you like it."

I couldn't help it. My stomach did a little flip and not just because I was hungry.

"So?" he said, watching me take a bite of toast. "Do you want to know what they have planned for you?"

I shrugged. As far as I was concerned, if it had to do with Trish's personal plans for Luke, the less I knew about it the better.

"What about you? Shouldn't you be more worried about what they've got planned for *you*?"

Luke looked at me for a minute, then turned away to clean the kitchen. I thought about pressing it, but ultimately decided I didn't want to know.

Luke had his back to me, putting the eggs back in the refrigerator, when he asked, "Have you ever kissed anyone, Micah?"

I looked down at my plate. "No."

It was silent for a bit, but when I looked up, Luke was facing me on the other side of the counter.

"Have you?" I asked.

"Tons of times." He grinned. "I can teach you if you want to practice for tonight." He wiggled his eyebrows.

I grabbed the wet dish towel sitting in front of me and threw it in his face as hard as I could.

"Hey!" He laughed.

I didn't know what made me madder, the fact that Luke had kissed Trish—tons of times, apparently—or the fact that he was teasing me about it.

The madder I got, the harder he laughed. Finally he held

up his hands. "There you go again with the laser beams. I was just kidding!"

"It's not funny," I said looking down. "I'm not kissing anyone, OK?"

"Fine."

We sat there silently for a minute, then Luke said, "Be honest, OK?"

"What?"

"Do you like Ryan?"

"I like Ryan a lot," I said. "He's always been really nice to me—even when you weren't." Luke looked down and started picking at his cuticles. "But I don't like him like that."

He chewed on his thumb for a minute before he spoke. "Well, I think he likes you."

I didn't say anything. I didn't know what to say. Nobody had really liked me like that before.

"If you don't really like him, we have to stop Ava and Trish before they do something that'll embarrass him," Luke said.

"Worse than yesterday, you mean?" I asked him.

"Yeah." He looked worried. "The guys and I talked about it yesterday after you both left. We filled Ryan in but . . . we don't want to tell you what our plan is. You might ruin it."

"How would I ruin it?"

"You'll act all weird."

"No, I won't!"

"Micah, you're a horrible liar. One look at your face and I can see everything you're thinking."

What? Crap! "That's not true!"

"It totally is." Luke smirked. "Look, just play along with the girls tonight. Do what they want you to do, even if it means letting them put makeup on you and stuff."

"No way! You saw how that turned out last time. Besides, how is that going to help with the plan?"

"Just trust me. The girls won't suspect anything if you play along. We'll take care of the rest. Now, let's go train."

"I thought we weren't training today. Isn't that what you told everyone else?"

"Do you want to make the team or not?"

"I told you from the beginning, I don't care about trying out."

"Well, do you care about beating Trish? She plays sweeper, just like you. You're better, though, and I think she knows it. That's why she doesn't want you on the team."

The idea of beating Trish was tempting. "OK, fine," I said, getting up and heading toward the backyard.

Who am I kidding? I thought as Luke dragged out the training equipment. I did want to make that team. It had nothing to do with the boys and everything to do with me.

I wanted to play. . . . I was just scared of what had happened the last time I was on a team.

What am I afraid of? I thought. *It's not like Libby will be there.* She, Samantha, and Marissa played in a totally different league. This was the perfect chance get a fresh start with a new team. I couldn't pass that up.

CHAPTER 29

49 days left

I spent all morning training with Luke.

"Use your left foot, Micah! You're wasting time switching to your right before you shoot. You've got to learn to use your weak side. . . . Try again." He passed the ball to me.

Frustrated, I kicked it with my left foot. The ball sailed toward Luke and nailed him in the stomach. "Oof!" He doubled over.

"Like that?" I asked, stifling a giggle.

"Yeah," Luke grunted. "Just like that."

After we were done, we snuck drinks from the water hose. I caught Luke watching me as I wiped the water off my face with the back of my hand.

"What?" I asked.

His eyes dropped. "Nothing." Then he grinned. "So are you ready for tonight? To get all done up?"

I scowled. "No."

He looked a bit concerned. "But you'll do it, right? For Ryan?"

"Of course," I said.

But Luke didn't look any less worried.

* * *

At six o'clock that evening, Dad and I were back outside the Waters's front door. I was about to ring the bell when the door swung open.

"Hey!" Megan said, pulling me inside. "Come on in." She grinned at my dad. "Hi, Mr. McKinney. My dad is in the backyard working on his dirt bike if you want to join him." Then she dragged me in the direction of her room. "And *you* are coming with me. We have a surprise."

As Megan carted me through the hall, we passed Luke's room. He stood in the doorway, and I shot him a pleading look, but he just winked and turned away, grinning to himself.

When we got to Megan's room, Trish and Ava were sitting on the bed with eager faces. I stopped dead in my tracks.

"Yay! She's here," Ava said clapping her hands together. "Micah, we're going to make you beautiful."

I tried to say something, but the only thing that came out was a weird "Uhhhuh." It sounded like air coming out of a balloon, which was exactly how I felt.

"Oh goodie." Trish grabbed her makeup bag.

"No, no," Megan said grabbing my arm again. "It's my turn." She gave me a pointed look that left me wondering if she knew what Trish had done the last time wasn't exactly her best work.

"Fine." Trish huffed. "But you have to look *extra* special for Ryan." She seemed a little too eager.

For once I didn't argue about not liking Ryan. I just played along like Luke had demanded. "OK," I said with a shrug.

Trish blinked. "OK?" I could tell she was thrown off by how quickly I'd given in.

"Yay! She's in!" Ava said, clapping her hands again. "You're not going to run off, are you?" she teased me. She turned to Megan. "Can I do her hair? Please!"

"First, let's pick out an outfit," Trish said, digging through a bag she'd brought. "I have just the thing for you."

"Sorry," Megan said, pulling me toward the closet. "I already promised Micah she could wear something of mine. We picked it out this morning."

We did? Megan looked at me long and hard, then gave one of those secret winks, so the other girls couldn't see. *Did Luke tell her about the plan?*

"This morning?" Trish asked, skeptical.

"Uh . . . yeah," I said, not really knowing where this was going.

"Cute! I love that watermelon bandeau," Megan said, looking at me in my jean shorts and white tank top. The bandeau showed through the arms of the loose top. "It'll go perfect with this dress." She pulled out a pink dress that complemented the watermelons. "But we need to get you some different shoes. Those red high-tops are all wrong."

"I don't know, they're kind of cute," Ava said. "In an old-school way."

I didn't know what to say. Spending the Fourth of July in a dress would be so uncomfortable. Luke had said to play along, but I wanted to enjoy the carnival rides—not worry about showing off my underwear.

"You know what?" I said, looking at the girls. "I think I'll just wear this."

Megan looked at me for a minute. "Are you sure?"

"Yeah, I'll be more comfortable."

She shrugged. "OK."

"But I still get to fix your hair," Ava said, running into the bathroom to turn on the curling wand before I could change my mind. "Right?" She looked at me. "Seriously, you can't run off. We have plans for you."

I stole a quick glance to where Trish sat pouting on the bed.

"No, I won't run away," I said, hesitating a bit. "Just . . .

don't make me look weird. OK?" Trish huffed an irritated breath. She must have known I was referring to her makeover skills.

"Got it!" Ava said, turning to face the mirror in the bathroom to apply more lip gloss.

"Ugh! This is so boring!" Trish whined. "I have nothing to do now." When nobody said anything she added, "Where's Luke? I think I'll hang out with him." Without waiting for a response, she walked through the bathroom and to his room.

I looked over at Megan, expecting her to roll her eyes, but she didn't. Instead, she ignored Trish and smiled at me. "Come sit over here so we can get started."

I did as I was told and closed my eyes while Megan applied makeup in light strokes. With Trish gone, I could feel myself relax for the first time since I had arrived.

While Megan did my makeup, Ava took to curling every hair on my head. "Geez you've got thick hair!" she complained as she finished twirling the last bit.

Neither of them would let me look in the mirror as Ava gently combed her fingers through my hair, trying to relax the curls. "Perfect," she finally said, looking down on me proudly. "OK, turn around and tell me what you think."

I braced myself for disaster, but when I saw myself in the mirror, my jaw dropped. I actually looked good—really good. My hair framed my face in all the right places, and my eyes sparkled. It didn't necessarily look like I was wearing makeup . . . my face just seemed to glow.

"Wow," I said. My eyes met Megan's reflection. "How are you so good at this?"

She shrugged. "It just takes practice. A little mascara and lip gloss and *vwah lah!*" she said with a flourish.

Ava ran her fingers through my hair one more time. The curls were now perfect waves that cascaded down my back. I looked like a mermaid. I stared at myself and touched a strand of hair. It was so soft and shiny. How had she done that?

"You look so good, Micah!" Ava said, looking at me through the reflection in the mirror. "I had no idea you were so pretty."

"Let's go show my mom, Micah," Megan said. "She's going to love it!"

We stepped through the door of Megan's room and out into the hall. As we passed Luke's room, my stomach flipped. Inside, Trish was sitting on the bed, watching Luke, Josh, and Ryan play video games. They all stopped what they were doing and gaped at me.

"Whoa, Micah!" Josh finally said. "You're hot! When did *that* happen?"

I laughed. "Shut up, Josh."

"Come on," Megan said, grabbing my arm. "Mom! Look what we did to Micah!"

Megan and Ava escorted me to the kitchen, where Sandi was prepping everything for dinner. Keaton was sitting at the breakfast bar munching on chips.

"What, hon?" Sandi asked, not looking up from what she was doing.

"Look what we did to Micah," Megan said again.

Sandi glanced up, distracted, then stopped what she was doing. "Oh! Micah, you look so beautiful!" She walked around the counter and squeezed me into a squishy hug, then pulled back and held me at arm's length. "Well, you're always beautiful but especially tonight."

I could feel the blood rushing to my cheeks. "Thanks."

Sandi turned to her son. "Keaton, can you tell the boys that dinner is almost ready?"

Keaton just sat there looking at me. "You look really pretty," he said shyly before heading back down the hall.

"Somebody's got a crush." Sandi winked at me.

"He's not the only one," Ava said, nudging me in the arm. "Ryan is going to lose his mind."

I gave a weak smile. Suddenly I didn't feel so good. I didn't want to do anything that was going to hurt Ryan's feelings.

Just then Nick slid open the glass door from the backyard. "Dinner ready yet?" he asked.

He stepped inside, followed by my dad, who stopped dead in his tracks when he saw me. Nick reached behind him to slide the door closed, stopping all the cool air from rushing out of the house.

"Oh," my dad said, flustered. "Sorry."

"The girls have been busy," Sandi said.

"I see that," Dad replied, walking toward me. He reached out and gave me a quick hug.

"Do you like it?" I was so nervous about what he thought.

Dad nodded, and his eyes sparkled a bit. "I do. You look beautiful . . . just like your mom."

CHAPTER 30

49 days left

We all ate dinner outside, the parents sitting at the patio table and the kids sprawled out in the grass. The whole time, I felt like I was on display. Every time I looked over at Ryan, he was watching me, and every time our eyes met, his ears turned red. Every time Luke or Josh made a comment about me, Trish would look over and glare.

Finally, when we were almost done eating, Trish asked, "When are we finally going to leave? I'm bored." When everyone ignored her complaining, she carried on. "My friends are waiting for me at the carnival already."

Megan and Ava exchanged glances, and Megan cocked her eyebrow. "What? We're not your friends anymore?"

But before Trish could reply, Sandi told us to clean up and get ready to go.

My dad handed me twenty bucks. "I think Nick and I are going to stay at the house a little while longer to finish working on the dirt bike. Are you all right if I meet you later at the fireworks?"

"Sure."

"OK, have fun, kiddo." He reached to muss up my hair like he usually did, but thought better of it and did an awkward wave instead.

When I turned around, everyone was already piling into Sandi's SUV. By the time I reached the door, there was nowhere for me to sit.

Trish smirked at me from her spot between Megan and Ava in the center row. "Looks like there's no room for you," she said.

"Oh no." Sandi turned around to study her back seats, which now looked like a clown car. "There aren't enough seats?"

"It's just right actually," I heard Trish mutter under her breath.

"Here, Micah," Ava said, squishing her body closer to Trish. "We can squeeze."

"Yeah . . . I don't think that's gonna work," Sandi said, trying to puzzle it out.

"Somebody can sit on my lap," Josh offered from the back row.

Sandi looked at him in the rearview mirror. "I don't

think so, buddy." She sighed. "Well, I guess we're going to have to take two cars."

"Why don't we just walk?" Megan chipped in. "It's a nice night."

"OK," Sandi agreed. "If that's what y'all want. I'll bring the blankets and chairs and you can just meet me there."

Trish rolled her eyes. It was clearly *not* what she wanted to do.

Everybody piled back out of the car, and we started off on the familiar walk to the high school, where we had played soccer nearly every day. Trish lagged behind, sulking and looking at her phone, probably texting her new friends to tell them about the lame new girl who'd made everyone walk.

At first I was walking between Megan and Ava, but somehow Luke and Josh wormed their way next to me.

"You're looking good tonight, Micah," Luke said, linking his arm into mine.

"Yeah, I think I might be in love," Josh said.

What the heck?

Luke gave Josh a pointed look. "Don't be so obvious," he whispered. I followed his eyes as they flicked back toward Trish, who was watching us.

"Who are you and what have you done with Josh?" I asked.

"I don't know what they did to you, but dang, Micah, you look *good*," Josh went on.

I could feel my face turning red.

"She did it for you, Ryan," Trish said, suddenly pushing her way to the front of the group. She shoved a hesitant Ryan toward me.

"Don't you think she looks pretty?" Ava asked him.

Ryan looked down at his feet and kicked a stray pebble. "She always looks pretty."

"Aw! That is so sweet!" Ava gushed.

When we turned the corner, I was amazed to see that the grounds of the high school had completely transformed. Both parking lots were covered with different rides and ticket booths. The closer we got, the giddier I became. We all walked together in an excited huddle toward the ticket booth, passing stalls smelling of popcorn and funnel cakes along the way. Music and squeals from kids on rides echoed through the air.

When we stepped up to the ticket booth, Trish's phone began to ring. She pulled it out of her pocket, eager to answer it. "Hello? Finally! I was getting so bored without you. . . . We're by the ticket booth. Where are y'all? Oh . . . OK, just meet us here. We'll wait for you."

She hung up the phone and turned to no one in particular. "Those were my friends from camp. They already scoped out some cute boys." She looked at Luke. "Not that I need it," she said. "Or you," she added, looking at me and gesturing toward Ryan.

"What about me?" Josh asked, holding his arms out. "I've been working out. Can't you tell?"

"EW!" Trish, Megan, and Ava shouted in unison.

Josh's face turned red, and he let his arms drop to his sides. He looked really sad, and for a moment, my heart broke for him.

"Come on," I said, grabbing his arm. "First ride is on me."

Josh turned to the guys and grinned. "Did you hear that? I get to sit with her first."

"Fine, but I've got the next ride," Luke said, holding up his tickets.

"Uh . . . hello?" Trish's eyes were bugging out of her head, and her jaw hung open.

Luke just shrugged. "What? Don't worry, Ryan will get his chance to ride with her too."

Trish looked to Ava, who gave her a pity shrug. Luke must have noticed it too, because he quickly said, "I thought you were meeting your friends at the ticket booth. Besides, I doubt you'd be able to keep up."

He motioned to the tall wedge sandals Trish had hobbled on our whole walk. They looked cute with her dress, but there was no way they were comfortable. I was glad to be in my sneakers. I'd break an ankle if I tried to wear those things.

"Give me a piggyback ride, Micah!" Josh said. He

suddenly grabbed my shoulders and jumped on without warning.

"What?" I screamed. I staggered, nearly falling on my face, but caught myself. *This is not what I meant when I said the first ride was on me.*

Luke laughed. "Now see if you can walk."

I could, but it was slow going as we made our way to the first ride. When I glanced back at the girls, Megan was smiling, and Trish and Ava were deep in conversation.

The first ride we came up to was one that spun around so fast that the riders got plastered to the walls of the circular cage. As soon as we got in line, I dropped Josh and turned to the boys.

"OK, what's up?" I asked over the people screaming on the ride.

"What do you mean?" Luke asked.

"Why are you guys acting all weird? Is this the plan?"

The boys all looked at me like they had no idea what I was talking about.

I used my best dude voice. "Looking good, Micah?" I mimicked. "And I think I'm in *love*," I added, punching Josh in the shoulder.

"Ow!"

"Yeah, OK, this is part of the plan," Luke admitted.

"What exactly *is* the plan?" I asked.

"We can't say," Luke said.

"Why not?"

All three boys looked at one another like they were trying to decide whether or not to tell me. Finally Luke said, "Actually *you're* kind of helping *me* out."

"How?"

"Well . . . the truth is, I never asked Trish to watch the fireworks with me. I just asked her if she was going. She must have taken it the wrong way, and now it doesn't matter what I say. I can't get her to go away."

I tried to hide the smile spreading across my face. If Luke didn't like Trish, then maybe there was a chance he liked me.

"She *is* hot though," Josh said.

"And annoying," Ryan added.

I rolled my eyes at Luke. "You do flirt with her, you know."

"No, I don't!" Luke protested.

"That's just the way he talks," Josh said.

That's certainly the truth, I thought.

"Anyway," Luke said, changing the subject, "I knew from snooping through Megan's messages that Trish was going to keep trying to set you up with Ryan. We thought the best way to get her off my back—and yours—was to pretend like the plan had worked too well and we'd all, like, fallen in love with you."

"Oh," I said, feeling a bit embarrassed.

So they were pretending to think I was pretty? I took the hair band off my wrist and piled my hair back on top of my head like normal. *Of course they were pretending. I'm such an idiot.*

"You wanna know the best part?" Luke asked. His eyes were bright with excitement.

"What?"

"We're all going to have a pretend fight over you on the soccer field," he told me.

"We even practiced," Josh said, looking just as excited.

I rolled my eyes. This plan was beyond dumb. "Why don't you just tell Trish you don't like her?"

Luke shrugged. "I don't know. It's kind of awkward."

"Yeah, well now you're putting *me* in an awkward situation."

"How?"

"Those girls already hate me."

"Megan doesn't," Luke said quickly. "And neither does Ava."

"Yeah, well Trish definitely does. And pretending like you're in love with me is just going to make her hate me even more."

"Who cares? You've got us," Ryan said. "If we do this, maybe she'll lay off. She's always trying to embarrass us."

I thought about all the times Samantha and Marissa had embarrassed me, making me look like an idiot in front of anyone who even considered being my friend. Then I thought about all the times Libby had just watched, never even once standing up for me.

"Girls can be horrible," I mumbled to myself.

"You're telling me," Josh agreed. "But man, do they look good sometimes."

He nodded behind us. I turned to see Megan, Ava, and Trish making their way over, but they weren't alone. Trish's new friends had joined their ranks. My stomach dropped when I realized who they were: Marissa, Samantha, and Libby—my former best friend.

CHAPTER 31

49 days left

The girls sauntered over in what I could have sworn was synchronized slow motion. All they needed to complete the look was a fan blowing their hair like in a music video. A part of me secretly wished one of them would trip on their tacky sandals and face-plant on the asphalt.

The girls stopped short when they saw me standing there. Libby looked almost as taken aback as I felt. Marissa's eyes bulged out, and within seconds she was whispering something in Samantha's ear.

I felt the blood drain from my body. I wanted to run, but I knew there was no escape.

Before anyone could speak, Luke grabbed my hand. "Come on, it's our turn!" He ran up the metal steps to the ride, dragging me behind him. Leaving the girls standing in our wake.

The other boys followed, and we all found our spots, spreading throughout the circular cage so we could see one another's faces. The ride started, and I let it spin me around and around until I forgot about the girls standing outside. They were probably salivating at the chance to make me miserable again.

By the time we got off, we were so dizzy and giddy that Ryan tripped going down the stairs. I grabbed one arm to hoist him up, and Luke grabbed the other as we all hunched over laughing.

I stopped laughing immediately when I spotted the girls walking toward us. "Come on," I said, tugging Ryan's arm harder than necessary. "Let's go!" I wanted to get out of there before they reached us. Those girls had a way of cutting me down to nothing, and I couldn't let them do that to me. Not in front of my new friends.

"You OK?" Ryan asked, looking at me like I was a weirdo.

"Let's go!" I shouted again at Josh and Luke.

"What's the rush?" Josh asked, eyeballing the girls as they made their way over.

It was too late. Trish ambled over, pulling up her strapless sundress. "Hey, guys, I want you to meet my friends from camp. This is Marissa and Samantha and . . . sorry, I forgot. What's your name?"

"Libby."

"Oh yeah, Libby." Trish smiled.

Libby and I briefly locked eyes, a leftover habit from years of friendship. In the past, we'd been able to have entire conversations simply by looking at each other . . . but we weren't linked up like that anymore.

"This is Luke," Trish said, giving the new girls a meaningful look. She must have told them about her date. "And this is Josh, Ryan, and . . . Micah." She said my name quickly, like it tasted bad.

Libby smiled and gave a timid wave, but Marissa huffed out a breath to show her disdain. I could see her watching the way my arm was linked through Ryan's. Her eyes narrowed as she zeroed in on her target, and I could tell she wasn't quite done with Operation: Make Micah Friendless.

Ryan must have noticed it too because he gave my arm a quick squeeze with his as it rested at his side. Luke rested his elbow on my shoulder, leaning into me.

Trish looked from me to Marissa. "Do you know each other?"

"I guess you could say that," Marissa said, twitching her nose.

Megan's eyebrows flicked up like they always did when she was about to get sassy.

"How do *you* know Micah?" Samantha asked, using her fake sweet-girl voice. I knew from experience that she was anything but. That was the voice she used before she chewed you up and spit you out.

"Micah just moved to our neighborhood," Megan cut in.

"Weird," Marissa said, all smiles. "We didn't even know you moved." She shot a glance at Samantha and Libby. Samantha giggled on cue.

"Really?" I asked, glaring back at them. "I could have sworn you knew. I got your going-away present."

Libby's eyes met mine, and for a brief moment, I thought I saw a flash of guilt. Then she looked down at her feet.

"It didn't fit, so I thought I would return it," I added, referring to the wad of wet toilet paper I had lobbed at Libby's window.

Marissa narrowed her eyes and glared at me. She knew exactly what I was talking about.

"*Well* . . . this has been fun," Luke said, obviously picking up on the tension. "But we've got stuff to do." He extended his arm around my shoulder and started to lead me away. "We'll catch up with you guys later," he added, looking at his sister.

"Wait for me," Megan said suddenly. She turned back to Ava. "Do you want to ride the Hammer Head with me?"

Ava shrugged. "Sure."

"But you're wearing dresses!" Trish reminded them.

Megan and Ava both lifted their dresses to reveal shorts underneath. "Didn't you wear shorts?" Ava asked.

Without another word, Trish stalked off, closely followed by her new soccer camp friends. Libby lagged behind, looking back at me for a moment before following too.

Once they were out of view, Luke let his arm drop as if it were now safe.

"Wow," Megan shook her head. "That Marissa girl . . ."

"Yeah," I muttered, not wanting to say anything else.

"How do you know her?" Megan asked.

"We used to be teammates," I confessed. There was more to it, but I wasn't about to get into that.

"Dang, Micah," Josh said, squirming his way between Megan and me. "You're worse with girls than I am."

"You're telling me," I mumbled.

"Well, apparently they're all trying out for Xpress," Megan said, sharing a worried look with Ava. "Trish told us while you guys were on the ride."

I stopped walking. "But they all play on the Strikers. Why would they try out for Xpress?"

"Trish said there was some kind of drama that made the coach quit," Megan continued. "I guess she stayed on for another year to see if she could find a replacement, but nobody volunteered, so the team folded."

Oh no.

I knew exactly what drama they were referring to. I knew, because I was the one who had caused it.

CHAPTER 32

49 days left

"You OK?" Megan asked. We stood next to the dunk tank where the boys took turns throwing baseballs. I didn't even remember walking there.

I blinked a few times, shaking myself from my thoughts. "Yeah, I'm fine."

I could tell she didn't believe me. Every now and then, Luke or Ryan would look over at me with a weird expression. It made me wonder what kind of face I was making. I tried to smile a bit more—I didn't want to ruin the night— but images of the last time I'd played soccer with those girls kept flooding my brain.

There's no way I can ever be on the same team as them again.

Eventually dusk came, and the sun started to set. We all headed back toward the soccer field to find a good spot to watch the fireworks. When we arrived, Trish and the other girls were already there waiting for us.

"There you are!" Trish linked her arm through Luke's as soon as she spotted him and led the way.

I tried to steer clear of Marissa, Samantha, and Libby as we walked, but Libby kept looking over at me, wearing the same face she always had when something was on her mind.

It wasn't long before we found the adults. Sandi had laid out a quilt for Keaton and Josh's younger brothers, and they were all coated in powdered sugar from the funnel cake they were sharing. My dad was sitting in a lawn chair next to Mr. Waters and another man who looked exactly like Josh, only with less hair.

"Hey, kiddo!" Dad said when he saw me. Then he noticed Libby with us. "And lookie there!" He got up to give her a hug. "I haven't seen you in forever," he added, giving her shoulder a quick squeeze.

"Yeah." Libby smiled kind of nervously.

"What have you and your mom been up to?" Dad asked. He looked around like he hoped he might spot her, and I forced myself to swallow down the bitter feelings starting to bubble up.

"Oh, nothing really." Libby shrugged shyly. "Just hanging around, I guess."

"Well, it's great to see you," Dad said, taking his seat again. "Tell your mom we said hi. We miss you guys."

Just then Megan leaned over to whisper in my ear. "Mom says you can spend the night if you want."

I looked at her, hesitant. I was not about to have a sleepover with Trish and the mean-girl brigade.

"It'll just be us," she assured me.

"OK, let me ask."

As the rest of the kids started walking off, I turned to my dad. "Megan wants to know if I can spend the night. Is that OK with you?"

"Sure, kiddo," he said. "And hey! How cool is that, seeing Libby? It seems like forever. First soccer, now Libby." He rubbed the top of my head proudly. "What a great night, huh?"

"Yeah," I said, trying to keep my smile from slipping. He wouldn't say that if he knew the truth. He just thought Libby and I had grown apart.

Luke turned around and waved me over. "Micah! Come on."

I looked up at my dad. "Go on, then," he said with another proud smile. I hurried after my friends, but behind me I heard Dad say, "And she's off. I hardly ever see that kid anymore."

"Join the club," Sandi said.

I caught up with the rest of the group, and we made our way toward the utility shed we had hidden behind at the start of summer.

"Our parents won't be able to see us here," Luke said, wiggling his eyebrows at me like he had earlier in the day.

I rolled my eyes but joined him in the grass as we all sat in a big circle waiting for the fireworks to begin.

"I've got an idea." Josh gave a devious grin to Luke. "Let's play Truth or Dare."

"Great idea," Luke said. "Who wants to go first?"

"Why don't you go?" Megan suggested.

"OK."

"Truth or dare?" she asked.

"Dare," he challenged with a smirk.

"I dare you to kiss Josh," Megan said.

We all laughed.

"Josh," Luke said, "as handsome as you are, buddy, I'm going to have to pass."

"Come on, Luke," Josh teased, rubbing his belly. "You know you want this."

Luke laughed. "No way! I'll do truth."

"That's no fair," Megan said. "I already know everything about you."

"No, you don't!" Luke protested.

"I know who you have a crush on," she taunted.

He looked at her as if to say, *You wouldn't.* Megan sat there, giving her brother a dose of his own signature smirk.

"Who is it?" Samantha finally asked, breaking the

silence. I could tell by the way she was looking at Luke that she wasn't immune to his charms either.

Megan didn't break eye contact with Luke. "I'll give you a hint. She's sitting in this circle."

I could feel my heart beat a bit faster. Then I looked over and noticed that Trish was having the same reaction.

"OK, this is lame," Marissa interrupted, taking over. "Micah, I dare you to kiss that guy." She pointed to Josh.

Josh immediately obliged. "OK," he said, crawling toward me through the circle.

"Oh no." This was not how I wanted to have my first kiss and not who I wanted it to be with.

"Aw, come on, Micah," Josh said. "Don't be such a baby."

The next thing I knew he was in my face.

"Don't you dare!" I warned.

But he kept coming closer—too close.

"Josh, stop!" I warned.

But he didn't listen, and before I could stop myself, I swung at him. I didn't mean to. It just happened. I landed a solid punch to Josh's mouth, and when I looked up, his lip was bleeding.

Everyone looked shocked, Josh most of all. "Crap, Micah!" he yelled. "What'd you do that for?"

Marissa smiled. This was the moment she'd been waiting for. "Because she's psycho." She looked right at me when she said it. "Just like her mom."

CHAPTER 33

49 days left

I couldn't breathe, and my hands were beginning to quake.

"Oh, what? You didn't know?" Marissa continued, looking around at everyone. "Her mom was flat-out crazy and—"

"Marissa!" Libby cut her off. "Stop."

"Shut up!" I screamed. Tears pooled in my eyes, threatening to spill over, and I bit my lip to keep it from trembling. I didn't know if I was going to crumble to pieces or explode, but if I didn't get out of here, it was all going to happen in front of everybody.

I took off running—away from the memories, away from the past that I couldn't seem to escape. I ran past the carnival rides, and down the sidewalk. I ran and ran, and by the time I got to my house, little animal noises were taking over as sobs wracked through my body.

I tried the handle on the front door, desperate to get inside, to not be seen, but it was locked. I banged my fist on the door in frustration. Being out in the open made me feel raw and exposed. I didn't know if anyone would follow me, but I knew I didn't want to see anyone. They probably all thought I *was* a psycho.

Panic was beginning to get the better of me. I gasped for air between waves of sobs, desperate to catch my breath. I was drowning in my own tears. Just when I thought I'd gotten a handle on it, a new wave would crush me and pull me under.

I rushed to the side of the house and scrambled to open my window, but the screen was in my way. I whipped around and saw the magnolia tree, holding its limbs out to me. All the blossoms had fallen off, but I could still smell its perfume.

Clinging to the branches, I climbed as high as I could go. Once I was safely hidden, I wrapped my arms around the rough bark of the trunk and pressed my face against the warm wood, just riding out the waves. I couldn't fight it anymore, I just let it wash over me as uncontrollable grief wracked through my body. I cried so hard, the whole tree shook. It must have scared the crickets because they quit chirping. The only sound was the echo of my own tears.

I wasn't sure how long I hid up there, but eventually I heard voices in my front yard.

"She's not answering the door." It was Megan.

"Come around this way. This is where her room is." Luke was with her.

"Creeper much?"

"Shut up. This is how I wake her up sometimes."

"That doesn't sound any less creepy."

They were walking underneath me now. I didn't want them to find me, but my breath kept wracking in my chest. There was no stopping it.

"Wait, do you hear something?" Luke asked.

"No."

"Listen . . ."

They got eerily quiet. I thought they might have left until I heard someone's cell phone ding.

"It's Mom," Megan said. "The fireworks are over, and she wants to know where we are. What do we say?"

"Just tell her that Micah is getting her stuff for the sleepover."

Megan's phone dinged again.

"Dang, Mom, calm down," Luke mumbled.

"It's actually Ava. She's mad that I left her with Trish and her new friends."

"Why don't you go back? I'll deal with this," he said.

"I don't think so."

"No, seriously, Megan. She was my friend first. You know that."

Megan sighed. "OK, fine. I'll see you at home."

I sat in the tree as quietly as I could, straining to hear if Megan had left. For a minute I thought Luke had gone too. Then I heard him say, "Move over, Micah. I'm coming up."

A moment later, he appeared on the other side of the tree trunk, about a foot away from me. The light from my neighbor's porch was blocked by the shade of the leaves, and all that remained were the flickers of green from the fireflies flitting around us in the dark.

"Hey," Luke said.

"Hi." I hiccupped.

"You missed the fireworks."

"I know."

We sat there for a little while longer, just watching the fireflies as they continued to blink on and off, on and off, until finally, the hiccups began to subside.

"Josh isn't mad at you, you know," Luke finally said.

I felt myself bristle. "I don't care," I lied. I couldn't stop picturing how hurt he'd looked after I'd hit him.

"Yeah, I figured." Luke sighed. "Just so you know, he wasn't entirely being a jerk. It was part of the plan. When one of us was dared to kiss you, that was what was supposed to start the fake fight. We just didn't plan on that Marissa girl being the one to issue the dare."

A gust of air hissed out of me at the mention of her name.

"And we weren't prepared for Josh being the one dared to do it." He looked at me and flashed his half grin. "Plus, we kind of forgot to calculate that you're like that freaking X-Men character who doesn't want to be kissed."

I *did* want to be kissed, just not like that. But I didn't tell him that.

We both sat in the quiet a bit longer. Eventually Luke asked, "So what's the deal with that girl anyway? Is she always like that?"

I shrugged.

"What she said . . ." Luke paused. "That was pretty messed up."

"Yeah," I agreed quietly.

Luke didn't say anything else. We just sat there, listening to the crickets as they regained their courage. He just sat there and waited.

Finally I whispered, "Maybe Marissa is right. Maybe my mom was crazy."

"What do you mean?"

I kept my eyes trained on a firefly. I couldn't look at him when I said it. "She killed herself," I whispered.

I felt Luke stiffen beside me. "Your mom committed suicide?"

I hesitated, but I couldn't stop it. The secret just kept on oozing out of me like a festering wound. "I've never told anyone before." I finally looked toward him in the dark. "*I'm* not even supposed to know."

We were both quiet then, and I thought of the things I had heard Mom say on those nights when she'd had too much to drink. I thought about the hurtful things she had written in her note. Was that even forgivable? I wanted it to be forgivable.

Then I thought of my own mean streak and sighed. "I can see how Marissa thinks I'm psycho too," I admitted.

"You're not psycho, Micah. And I can't believe anyone thinks you are."

I sighed. *He won't say that he once he knows what I did.*

CHAPTER 34

When Mom died, everything changed all at once. Libby's mom was devastated. We all were. I felt so alone. Libby would still come over from time to time, but Kristen never came with her. It was like that for months. Then one day after soccer practice, Dad invited them both over for pizza, and a little bit at a time, life started to feel normal again—a new kind of normal.

At first I loved the new routine, but then things started to get weird. Every now and then Libby and I would walk into the living room, and we could tell from their splotchy faces that Dad and Kristen had been crying together.

Seeing them like that always made my stomach twist. I didn't know why. I should have been glad my dad had someone to talk to, but the way they were acting just felt private and personal. It made me feel like an intruder in my own home.

Dad had enrolled me in some sort of therapy program at school, where I'd get pulled from lunch every now and then to talk to a counselor while I ate. We'd sit in a small room, and I'd pick at my peanut-butter-and-jelly sandwich while the counselor smiled politely and waited for me to answer her questions. It stressed me out more than anything else.

I couldn't tell her how I was doing because I couldn't tell her what I knew. She assured me that everything I said would be confidential, but every time I thought of what I really needed to say, I remembered the broken look on my dad's face when I'd tried to talk about it. Nobody could know what I knew. It would shatter him.

Every day Libby saved me a seat at lunch. And every day I kept my head down and pretended like I didn't see her. I didn't want to talk to anyone. I *couldn't* talk to anyone, even Libby. There was just too much I couldn't say. I couldn't tell Libby I hated it when her mom came to my house, and I hated the way she looked at my dad. I couldn't tell her that I wished they would stop coming over altogether because it made me miss my mom even more. I couldn't tell her the truth: that my mom had killed herself and sometimes I worried I had done something to make her leave. That if I had just done one thing differently, she might still be here.

I couldn't tell her any of that. So instead I avoided her and hoped the feelings would go away. But they never did.

Tired of being left alone, Libby started to hang out at Marissa's house more and more. She stopped saving me seats at lunch and started eating at the popular table with Marissa and Samantha. And when I didn't joke around with her at soccer practice anymore, she convinced Marissa to join our team.

As the time passed, things didn't get any better. They only got worse.

The weekend before the incident, Libby and her mom came over after our soccer game. It had been a while since I'd seen them. I had started disappearing on bike rides or hiding out in trees whenever they came over, and eventually Libby stopped coming. Things had gotten even weirder between us. We didn't talk much that night and ended up falling asleep to a movie in my room.

It was late when I woke up feeling thirsty. I went to get a drink of water, and that's when I found them—Libby's mom and my dad—in the kitchen. My mom's kitchen. My dad had his arms wrapped around Kristen—my mom's best friend, my soccer coach. She was standing there with her arms wrapped around him too, resting her cheek against his chest.

My breath caught in my throat, and my ears started to

ring. The moment was intimate—too intimate. And more than that, it was a betrayal.

I silently turned around and walked away. I didn't breathe the whole way back to my room, afraid I might scream. I could feel the white-hot rage pulsing behind my eyes as I blinked back the tears. I hated them both. At least I wanted to. I couldn't hate my dad. He was all I had left.

I never told Libby what I saw. It was just one more thing that I kept to myself, another secret shoved down deep inside.

But it must have been one secret too many because something in me changed. I could feel it. It was like a seed had been planted and ugly roots were growing deep, taking over the whole of me. What had been disbelief turned into resentment and then finally festered into a full-blown rage. I was infected with hate, because hate felt better than hurt.

At our final practice near the end of fifth grade, Libby and Marissa showed up together—again. They had apparently spent the day getting ready for a slumber party Marissa was throwing on the last day of school. I'd overheard Marissa earlier that week, debating on who was cool enough to go and who wasn't. I hadn't made the cut.

I watched them together while I tied my cleats, wishing I could work up the courage to talk to Libby. I glanced down for a moment, and when I looked up again, I was surprised to see Libby and Marissa watching me from across the field.

I waved, and Libby gave me a half wave back. I expected Marissa to ignore me, like usual, but she just stood there looking at me, long and hard. It was weird. She had never looked at me like that before.

I decided right then that time was up. I couldn't just let Libby go. I *had* to talk to her. I just didn't know where to start. I wanted to apologize for pushing her away, even though she'd always been a good friend to me. I wanted to tell her that I missed her. I wanted things to go back the way they were.

I took a deep breath and walked over to where they were standing. Both Libby and Marissa had their backs to me as I approached, but that didn't stop me from overhearing.

"How sad," Marissa whispered. She lowered her voice even more. "I can't imagine what I would do if my mom did that. Why would a mom kill herself?"

I stopped in my tracks. How did she know that? Nobody was supposed to know. *I* wasn't even supposed to know.

They both turned, and Libby's face paled when she saw me standing there. "Micah . . . ," she began.

I backed away from her, then turned and walked off, feeling numb, and trying to catch my breath.

"You OK, Micah?" Kristen asked as I walked past.

I looked up at her, and that's when I knew. It was *her*. It must have been. *She* was the one who had told Libby about my mom. *She* was the reason Marissa now knew too.

I looked away, but I could still hear my heartbeat thrumming through my ears. With each *thump*, the anger pulsed through me like a poison.

The longer practice went on, the angrier I got. The angrier I got, the harder I played. Libby tried to talk to me a few times, but I brushed her off. She didn't exist as far as I was concerned. It didn't help that Marissa kept darting pity looks in my direction. She had never been nice to me before. Why would she start now?

I hated knowing they'd been talking about me—talking about my mom. Talking about things they had no business talking about—saying things *I* wasn't even allowed to say.

During our final water break, it all came to a head. Kristen was talking to Libby and Marissa, and all at once, they looked up at me, identical masks of pity on their faces.

Before I could stop myself, I slammed my foot into the ball in front of me, sending it flying in their direction. I didn't care who it hit. I just wanted it to hit someone, to wipe that look off their faces.

I watched it plummet toward them and saw Marissa's eyes widen when she realized the ball was going to slam into her face.

An instant later, Kristen was by my side, grabbing my shoulders. "Micah!" She made me face her. "Why did you do that? What were you thinking?"

I shoved her away furiously. "Get off me!" I screamed at

her. I took a breath, and everything I had been holding onto came pouring out—rage I didn't know I had in me.

Kristen kept hold of my shoulders, trying to calm me down, but I couldn't stand to have her touch me. I kicked and hit and screamed with everything I had. I wanted Kristen to hurt. I wanted her to feel the betrayal that I felt, that my mother would have felt.

When it was over, Kristen and I were left sitting on the field, covered in dirt. I was out of breath, and my throat was raw from screaming. The whole team was staring at us with wild eyes. Nobody knew what had gotten into me.

I stopped talking to Libby completely after that. Or she stopped talking to me. It didn't really matter which. It was like we had never been friends. I was friendless, but I told myself that I didn't care. As long as Libby stayed away, so did her mom.

I was sure Kristen would call at some point to tell my dad what had happened—what I'd done—but the call never came. It wasn't until a month later, when I was outside checking the mail, that Kristen pulled her Jeep up to the curb. Dad was at work, and I wondered if she had planned it that way.

"Micah!" she called from her window. She winced when I turned to look at her. The hate I felt must have been etched all over my face. "Micah, I'm sorry. I never meant to hurt you. *We* never meant to hurt you."

I stepped toward her. "You and my dad are not a WE. They were a WE, he and my mom."

Kristen looked at me, stunned. "I was talking about Libby and me. Libby told me what happened. What you heard. I'm so sorry. I only told her because she was so sad, she didn't understand—"

I didn't want to hear it, and I didn't want to talk about it. Not with her. I turned away again and walked back toward the safety of the house.

"Micah . . . wait!" Kristen called after me.

I stopped walking but didn't turn around.

"Your dad doesn't know what happened at practice . . . or what you overheard. But I think you should talk to him, Micah."

I whipped around. "About what? My dead mom or the fact that you're trying to take her place?"

"What?" Kristen looked stricken.

"Don't play dumb. I saw you together in the kitchen."

"Micah, it's not like that—"

"I know what I saw!" At least I thought I did. Could I have been wrong? No. I definitely saw them together.

"Micah . . ." Kristen sighed. "Your dad and I are just friends. We both miss your mother—so much. I know you do too. But I'll give you some space, if that's what you need."

I didn't know what to say. I didn't want time. I missed

Libby already, but I couldn't stand the thought of her mom being with my dad.

For a moment, it looked like Kristen was going to leave, but then she said, "You don't have to quit soccer over this. I'll quit. I'll find a new coach for the team. You can stay, and things can go back to the way they were."

I didn't respond. I just turned around and walked inside, letting the door slam behind me. It was too late. Things would never go back to the way they were. The damage was done.

CHAPTER 35

49 days left

Luke and I sat in the darkness of the magnolia tree a bit longer. It was the most I'd ever told anyone. Without warning, he reached across the branch we were both leaning against and put his hand on mine.

"Is that why you quit playing soccer?" he finally asked.

I nodded, feeling the warm tears of regret build up again. My voice cracked when I finally spoke. "I broke her nose," I confessed.

"Marissa's?"

"Yeah. Libby thought I did it on purpose. I could tell by the way she looked at me. All the girls did, and they all thought I was psycho because of it."

I looked down at my dangling feet. *Maybe I was psycho.* Then I thought about Josh and his cut lip. *Maybe I am.*

"Marissa had to wear a weird-looking nose cast thing on the last day of school. Everybody knew I did it, and nobody would talk to me after that. It sucked, but I deserved it."

Luke was quiet for a long time. Finally he said, "I'm sorry about your mom, Micah."

I hated it when people said that. "Sorry for what? I don't want you to feel sorry for me, Luke." A hiccup wracked through my body again. "I shouldn't have even told you."

He took his hand away from mine, and I instantly felt bad. "Well, I'm glad you told me," he said softly. "Even if you're not."

Loneliness washed over me, and I wanted to reach out to him, to hold his hand again, but I was scared. What if he pulled away? Hesitantly I reached out and placed my hand on top of his. Relief washed over me when he wrapped his warm fingers around mine and gave a quick squeeze. I was forgiven.

I sighed. "Well, I guess this is it. You don't have to come by in the mornings anymore because I'm not trying out for the team."

"What? Why?"

"There's no way I can try out for Xpress now. Those girls won't want to play with me, and to be honest there's no way I want to be on a team with them after all that."

"Look, if you just don't want to play soccer that's one thing." Luke turned to face me. "But if you're wimping out because you're scared of what those girls think of you, that's another." I could feel him looking at me, long and hard. "What do you want, Micah? Do you want to play or not?"

I was silent for a long moment. I did want to play, and not just because that meant Luke would keep knocking on my window every morning or because it would make my dad happy. I wanted to play for me.

Before I could answer him, Luke's phone began to buzz in his pocket. "It's Megan," he said. "Our parents are starting to worry about us."

"OK."

"Megan wants to know if you still want to spend the night. She said Ava wants to stay too and was wondering if you cared."

"No Trish?"

"No Trish. No Marissa, either."

"OK, let me go get my stuff."

* * *

As we made our way to his front door, Luke stopped and turned to me. "Just so you know, Josh and Ryan are spending the night too."

"Oh," I said, feeling my stomach lurch a little. Despite what Luke had said, I was still kind of scared that Josh would be mad at me.

"Megan and Ava will probably hog you the rest of the

night." Luke looked at me. "And Ryan will probably be mad at me for running after you. He wasn't pretending tonight, you know. He won't admit it, but he really does like you." He shoved his hands in his pockets and looked down.

"Were *you* pretending?" I asked before I could stop myself. I immediately wanted to take it back.

Luke looked up and flashed a crooked grin. "Can't say. I don't want a busted lip." Then he walked into the house.

* * *

In the safety of Megan's room, I told her everything I had shared with Luke. The mistakes I had made and the things I had done and the friendship I had lost. I let her see the ugly parts of me and shared the things I had always tried to hide. And like a good friend, she just listened.

Ava arrived just as we were wrapping up. "Whoa . . . you two look so serious," she said, walking into the room. "What y'all talking about?"

"Nothing," Megan said quickly.

Ava's face dropped a bit. I didn't want to be the reason she felt left out, so I said, "I was just explaining why those girls hate me."

Ava sat down on the bed next to me.

"It's a long story," I said.

"I get it." Ava smiled. "You don't have to tell me."

I smiled back. "Thanks."

"But if they mess with you again, just know that we've got your back."

I couldn't help the tears that sprang up.

"Don't cry!" Megan wrapped her arms around me.

"Ahhh!" Ava smothered Megan and me in a bear hug until we all toppled off the bed in a tangled heap of giggles and tears.

That's when Luke opened the door. "What's going on in here?"

Ryan popped his head in behind Luke to check it out too.

"Get out!" Megan yelled.

Josh barged his way in. "Sweet!" he said, charging toward us. "DOG PILE!"

Luke and Ryan followed suit and piled on top of us until everyone was laughing and gasping for air. Eventually we ended up sitting in a huddled circle on the floor next to Megan's bed, just like we had on the soccer field earlier that night.

Josh looked at us all and cocked his eyebrow. "So . . . who wants to play Truth or Dare?"

We all threw pillows at him. "No way! Are you crazy?"

After everyone settled down, I hugged the pillow in my lap a little harder, and nudged Josh with my shoulder. "I'm sorry," I whispered, ". . . about earlier."

He smiled and shoved me back, making me tip over.

"Me too." I looked up at him and giggled, but his eyes were serious. "I should have backed off."

I could feel Luke looking at me from across the circle. "So how about it, Micah?" he said. "Are we training tomorrow or not?"

I could see the challenge in his eyes, waiting and unspoken. Was I going to try out for the team, or was I going to quit? As I stared at him, I felt my stubborn sense of determination begin to bubble up.

Fifty days. That's all I have left before the first day of school and my thirteenth birthday. Who do I want to be at the end of that?

I looked Luke in the eye and smiled. "Oh, we're training," I said. "We're definitely training."

Luke's face broke out into a huge grin, and I couldn't help it, my heart melted a little.

Just then Sandi stuck her head through the doorway to see us all mixed together and said, "All right, it is getting *way* too late for this nonsense. Time to break it up. Boys, backyard campout. Girls, you stay inside. Now all of you, get to bed."

CHAPTER 36

17 days left

I lost track of time as the rest of the month flew by. Each day was a blur of sweaty soccer sessions and hours at the pool. Trish wasn't around as much, and with her gone, Ava and Megan joined the boys and me in our shenanigans. Long days were followed by late nights spent walking around the neighborhood. We mostly just talked, but sometimes we'd play games like flashlight freeze tag. If it was particularly hot, we'd raid random yards, looking for sprinklers to cool off in.

I tried to think of what my summer would have been like if the boys hadn't caught me drooling in the grass that first day. What would it have been like if they hadn't challenged me at the pool? If Luke hadn't show up at my window and convinced me to join the soccer team?

Tryouts were the next day, and we had just wrapped up our last training session. I looked over at the boys, currently drinking from the water hose in Luke's backyard. I couldn't imagine what summer would've been like without them.

I had to do well tomorrow. I wanted more than anything to make those boys proud. To thank them for all that they had done for me and prove that it was all worth it, that I wasn't a waste of time.

* * *

The day of tryouts I woke up early, but stayed in bed for a long time, just blinking up at my ceiling. Finally I rolled over and looked at the calendar on my wall. There were less than three weeks of summer vacation left.

Sixteen days until I turn thirteen. Sixteen days until school starts.

What would it be like once school started? Would the boys still want to hang out with me? Would Megan or Ava? What were we going to do when we didn't have soccer to train for or the pool to go to?

Just then I heard the familiar tapping outside my window and felt myself relax. I opened my curtains, surprised to see not only Luke, but Josh and Ryan as well. They were all grinning at me through the screen like a bunch of idiots.

Josh pushed in between Luke and Ryan. "Wake up!" he shouted. "Today's the day! We've got to get you fueled up."

Luke pushed him back and smiled at me. "You want to come over? Mom's making waffles."

I smiled and hopped out of bed. There was nowhere else I'd rather be.

We ended up hanging out at the Waters's house all day, playing video games and then doing backflips on the trampoline. I was having so much fun I forgot to pay attention to the clock, and when I looked at it again, I was shocked to see that it was 3:26. Tryouts started in an hour.

"Crap! I've got to go home!"

I raced home and gathered all my gear—including the new cleats Dad had insisted on buying me, and my bigger ball. As soon as he got home from work, we were out the door, driving with the windows rolled down. I could feel Dad looking at me every now and then, and it made me even more anxious. I tapped my foot while we sat at the red light just outside the parking lot.

"I'm so glad you're doing this, Micah," Dad said as the light turned green and he pulled into the parking lot. "I've really missed watching you play."

I was too nervous to respond.

As soon as he parked the truck, I turned to get out, but Dad said, "Hey, wait a minute. Look at me." He waited for me to face him. "You're going to do great. No matter what happens, I'll be proud of you." I nodded, and he reached for the door like he was about to get out but stopped. He leaned back in his seat and looked over at me. "Your mother would have been proud too, Micah. She loved to watch you play."

I nodded again and tried my best to smile, but Dad's words threw me. We hardly ever talked about Mom, and suddenly I wanted to cry. I tried to swallow, but my mouth was too dry.

My new cleats felt weird and clunky on my feet as I walked up to the group of girls gathered in the center of the field. They chatted with one another and passed the ball around while they waited for tryouts to begin. Megan and Ava both greeted me as soon as I arrived and passed me the ball to include me in their warm-up circle.

I couldn't help noticing that Trish was on the other side of the field with her new friends instead of with Ava and Megan. She saw me looking and gave me one of her fake smiles. Libby was sitting with them too, a little off to the side. She looked up and our eyes met, but I looked away.

"Why is Trish over there?" I asked.

Megan just shrugged her shoulders.

"Apparently she's too good for us now," Ava said bitterly.

"That's not true," Megan said. "She's just being a brat because Luke doesn't want to be her boyfriend."

I glanced back across the field to see Trish staring at the sidelines where some of the boys had gathered to watch. When I followed her gaze, it led directly to Luke.

"You've got this, Micah!" he yelled, waving at me.

The other guys joined in and pumped their fists. "Ka-hu-na! Ka-hu-na!"

I looked at Trish again and flinched. She was glaring at me as the boys continued to chant.

Just then, two coaches waved us over to the center of the field. "OK, bring it in, ladies," one of them hollered.

We all hustled over and took seats on the grass while the coaches introduced themselves.

"As many of you know, I'm Coach Tremble," the coach continued.

"Coach T!" some of the girls chanted.

He smiled. "Otherwise known as Coach T. I'm the head coach. Our new assistant coach is unavailable tonight, so Coach Katney from the boys' team is here to help."

Coach Tremble carried on with his spiel about what the club was looking for in their players. I tried to pay attention, but behind him I could see Josh doing some sort of weird dance. The boys were all hunched over, cracking up.

I scanned past them to the clump of parents and spotted my dad standing off to the side by himself. He gave me a thumbs-up when he caught me looking.

What a dork. I smiled back.

Then suddenly I spotted her—Kristen. She was standing on the other side of the bleachers, chatting animatedly with some of the other moms.

The breath left my lungs. Why hadn't I thought about

her being here? Of course she would be here to support Libby.

I hadn't seen her in nearly a year, and I cringed remembering how *mean* I'd been to her that day outside my house. But even so, I couldn't help feeling a little bitter that my mom wasn't over there with her.

Just then Kristen looked up and saw me staring. She hesitated for a moment, then gave a timid wave. I turned my head away, pretending to not see her.

My stomach churned, and I couldn't tell if it was from hunger or guilt. Maybe I should have eaten something beforehand, but I was pretty sure I'd be puking now if I had.

I glanced across the field to where Libby sat and was surprised to see her now even farther way from her friends than before. Marissa and Samantha, meanwhile, were huddled together, whispering to Trish. They nodded in my direction, and Trish gave me a look I couldn't quite place. It felt like déjà vu.

Great. There's no telling what they're saying.

Finally it was time to move. I could feel some of the jitters leave my body as we went through the warm-up: jogging around the field, high-knees, butt kickers, side skipping on both sides. Then we broke up to do some skills, followed by shooting drills.

Things were going pretty well. The boys' coach had even come by and complimented me at one point. I was feeling good until Coach T announced it was time for three-on-three. I was paired up with two girls I didn't know, and when I looked across the makeshift pitch to see who we were playing my body went stiff. Marissa was glaring at me on the other side of the field.

Awesome.

When I glanced over at the sidelines, things only got worse. My dad had made his way to Kristen's side, and they were leaning toward each other as they talked and watched us play.

I could feel the anger start to creep up again. *Why can't he just stay away from her? What are they even talking about?*

Then a horrible thought hit me. What if they weren't just catching up? I thought about the last time Kristen and I had been on a soccer field together, and I began to wonder what she *had* told Dad after that final practice.

She had to tell him something. *What was her explanation for not coming over anymore?*

A parent volunteer blew the whistle, and we got started, but I was off-kilter. My feet tangled beneath me, and I couldn't concentrate. I ended up staying back and defending the goal for the most part as I tried to get my bearings back.

From behind me I heard Luke shout, "Come on, Micah! What are you doing? Get in there!"

But I couldn't. The other team was totally dominating

us. During the next play, Marissa came forward with the ball. She'd been a defender on the Strikers, so I was surprised to see her make her way to the goal. She didn't pass it to any of the other players on the team but continued straight at me.

I ran toward her to fend her off, and she elbowed me in the ribs, shoving me off the ball. It knocked the breath out of me, and I was taken aback. She glared at me and did it again and again.

With each nudge, my temper rose higher and higher, but I resisted the urge to charge at her like I wanted to. Instead I took my time, covering her every move.

Finally, when the time was right, I snatched the ball away and dribbled up the field. I dodged defenders, using the footwork I'd been working on with the boys during our training sessions.

"YEAH!" Josh shouted behind me.

As I neared the goal, Marissa caught up and covered me tightly on my right side. I took aim with my left foot, just like Luke and I had practiced, and felt it connect with the ball. I knew right away it was a clean shot—the ball sailed into the back of the net as the coaches blew the whistle to indicate that it was time to huddle up again.

The boys cheered from the sideline. "See? That's how you do it!" Luke shouted.

Marissa scowled at me as I walked toward Ava and

Megan, feeling proud. I scanned the parents on the sidelines again to get Dad's reaction to my shot, but when I found him, my smile faded. He was still standing next to Kristen, maybe even a little closer now, and clearly hadn't even seen my goal. I clenched my fists. They were too busy talking.

I couldn't help thinking of my own mom. She'd always been the loudest one there, always cheering me on. Well, maybe not always, but if she were feeling well she would have been. When she was fully *there*, I had her full attention. When she wasn't . . . well, she wasn't. I tried not to think about the times when she'd been too tired to get out of bed. When she'd been having one of her bad days and just wanted to be left alone.

I looked over at Dad again. Despite all that, I wished Mom was standing there with him. I wished she could have been here to see how good I'd gotten. It should have been her standing by his side instead of Kristen.

I started to feel that empty feeling again and tried to ignore it. The coaches told everyone to line up to do shooting drills next, and before I knew it, it was my turn. It was the last drill, and I had just shanked a ball over the net when Trish snuck up behind me.

"Don't worry, Micah," she said, startling me. "It's OK if you don't make the team. I mean . . . it's not like it's anything to kill yourself over."

With that, she smiled and jogged away. Only it didn't look like a smile. It looked like a slap in the face.

I watched her jog back up to Marissa and Samantha; they all looked at me and laughed. I just stood there, feeling myself crumple from the inside out.

Now Trish knows? Who else did they tell?

Megan stepped closer with a concerned look on her face. I hadn't even realized she was so close. "What did she just say to you?"

"Nothing." I tried to shake it off, but it felt like the air had been let out of me. I couldn't move right. Girls juked past me, and I kept losing control of the ball. Everything was slipping out from underneath me.

I could hear my dad on the sidelines. "That's OK, Micah! Just shake it off, kiddo!"

Oh, now he pays attention.

I looked over at the coaches, who were jotting down notes on their clipboards, probably scratching my name off the list. I looked over at the boys, who were watching me quietly, no longer cheering, and I could see their disappointment from across the field. I was letting them down. I could see it on their faces.

Then I looked over at my dad again, just in time to see him throw his head back and laugh at something Kristen had said. He patted her on the back, gripping her shoulder and giving it a quick squeeze.

I could feel the anger rearing its ugly head again. If Dad would stop flirting for two seconds he'd see that I needed him.

I couldn't stop the tears that welled up, threatening to spill over. I couldn't take any more. This whole thing was a mistake—a big, big mistake.

I just took off running, right in the middle of a play. At first it looked like I was running after the ball, but then I ran past the goal and kept going.

Behind me, I heard a confused Megan shout, "Micah? Where are you going?"

I ignored her and everything I was leaving behind. I just focused on the sound of my cleats hitting the sidewalk and my breathing as I ran. I ran as fast as I could. I ran all the way home—to my old home.

CHAPTER 37

17 days left

It was getting dark by the time my dad's truck pulled up to the curb. I'd wanted to sit on my old porch swing, but things had changed since the last time I'd been there. A new family had moved in, and some other kid's bike was lying on its side in the front yard under the old oak tree where my bike used to lie.

I didn't look up when Dad shut off the engine or even when he sat down next to me. We just sat there for a minute, listening to the crickets and the cicadas and Mrs. Sanders's annoying dog barking a few houses down.

Finally Dad spoke. "What happened, kiddo?"

I kept my eyes glued to the asphalt, clenching my jaw.

"Come on. Talk to me."

It was like I'd been holding my breath, and suddenly I couldn't hold it for another second. "I saw you with her," I blurted out.

"What? With who?" Dad seemed confused, like he had no idea what I was talking about.

I refused to look at him. "Kristen."

"Yeah, Libby was trying out too—"

"Not today. Last year, in the kitchen . . . I saw you holding her." My voice cracked on the last word. I hadn't realized I was crying until that moment.

I heard a quick intake of breath and then a long exhale, as if Dad were trying to blow away the words I'd just said. "It's not what you—"

I kept talking, even angrier now. "You were both in *Mom's* kitchen, just holding each other like she never even existed. Like nothing ever happened!"

As soon as it was out, I wished I could take it back. I knew it was a low blow. I didn't even know why I'd said it. *What did I just do? Why am I so mean?*

Dad took in a shaky breath. "Micah. It's . . . complicated. Your mother was . . . complicated."

The wall inside me burst, and it felt like I was drowning in a wave of tears. I didn't try to hold it back this time. I just let it wash over me.

"Why?" I asked, wading my way through the sobs. "Why did she leave us? Why didn't she love us?" I stopped to catch my breath and managed to whisper the last question. "What did we do wrong?"

Dad grabbed my shoulders firmly and made me face him. "Look at me. We did nothing wrong, Micah. It was not us, honey. It was her." He suddenly sounded broken. He dropped his hands and looked forward. "I couldn't help her. I tried, but she had to help herself."

"I read her letter," I said quietly. "I know I shouldn't have but . . . I found it in the trunk. She was so mean. Why would she say all those awful things?"

Dad sighed. "I don't know, Micah. Sometimes she said things that she didn't mean. We both said and did things we would regret. She got like that sometimes, so I just left her alone to calm down and the next thing I knew . . ." He looked down. "She was gone."

Gone. We both felt it—the empty, hollow feeling of being left behind—and we just sat there together and cried. I didn't know how it happened, but suddenly I was in Dad's lap and he was squeezing me tight. I couldn't tell where his tears ended and mine began.

Finally, after he'd gotten ahold of himself, Dad said, "But you need to know, nothing happened with Kristen. We were both missing your mother so badly, and I don't know . . . it just felt good to be around someone who'd known her. Who actually understood her."

That's when I told him. I told him everything. How I'd

caught Libby talking about Mom and how I'd lost it and broke Marissa's nose. About all the hate I'd felt and how mean I'd been to Kristen.

When I was finished, I turned to him. "I'm sorry. I pushed Kristen away. I don't blame you for wanting to talk to somebody. I don't want you to be alone. It's just . . . I'm not quite ready for you to be with anyone yet."

Dad sighed. "Believe me, kid, I'm not ready for that either." He looked down at his hands and then up at me again. "I'm sorry too," he said. "I'm sorry for not being up front about your mom. I just . . . I didn't know what to tell you."

"You didn't want to tell me she was crazy because I might be just like her," I said, mostly to myself.

His face crumpled. "Oh, Micah . . . you're not crazy, and neither was your mom. She was sick. She suffered from an illness that affected the way she saw the world sometimes. Depression can make people do crazy things, but she wasn't crazy. She loved you more than anything."

"She loved you too, Daddy."

He buried his head in my neck, and I knew he was crying again, but for the first time it didn't scare me. I just squeezed him until he was done.

Eventually Dad looked at me again, trying to smile through his tears. "You know, Micah, it's OK to be sad. You know that, right? Everyone gets depressed from time to time. It's a part of life, but it's all in how we handle it. You have to face your emotions instead of hiding from them. Otherwise, they just kind of eat you up inside."

I nodded.

Dad took in a deep cleansing breath and wiped his eyes with the palms of his hands. "Well, kid, this is where it stops. We don't hold back from each other anymore. We have to talk." He tried to smile again, but it wavered. "I know you try to protect me sometimes, just like I try to protect you. But we need to face this head-on. We're all we've got, so we have to stick together. We have to be honest with each other."

I nodded my head. "OK."

"I love you so much." He squeezed me again. "I'm so sorry. I had no idea you were going through all that."

I could feel my body relax in his arms. "Me either," I whispered.

CHAPTER 38

9 days left

I laid low for the next week. Every morning the boys would knock on my window, and every morning I ignored them. I was too ashamed to face them. To face how I'd blown it. After all that work they'd put in helping me train . . . they would know it had been a waste of time. That *I* was a waste of time.

I hadn't talked to Megan and Ava either. There was no telling what they thought of me after I'd run off like that. I didn't know what was wrong with me. Why did I keep doing that?

I was driving myself crazy staying holed up in the house. Being inside made me irritable, and my legs twitched from not training. But mostly I was just disappointed. I hadn't realized how badly I'd wanted to make the team. I needed to play, but I had ruined my only chance. I'd thrown it away, and there was no turning back.

Finally, it was Saturday, and there was only a week of summer vacation left. The minutes ticked by, eating away at the time. All those days had gone by and what did I have to show for it? I was in exactly the same situation I'd been in at the beginning of summer—pathetic and friendless.

Suddenly there was a knock on the door, and I looked across the dinner table to where Dad sat, washing down our late dinner of spaghetti with a glass of iced tea. He gave me the same look he'd been giving me for the past few days. "You going to let me answer the door yet?"

I looked down at my spaghetti. Being brave was easier said than done.

"You know he's not going to give up, right? It's only fair to put him out of his misery."

I still didn't say anything.

There was another, more urgent, knock on the door.

"That's it." Dad's fork clattered onto the plate as he stood up. "I can't let you do this again. You can't stay inside forever, you know. You need to talk to him."

I just sat there, twirling the spaghetti I didn't plan on eating, as I heard the door open.

"Well, well . . . if it isn't Luke Waters," Dad said. "Come on in, kid. She's at the table."

A moment later, Luke walked into the kitchen. I looked

up at him, trying to decide if he was angry or not by the look on his face, but I couldn't tell. I waited for him to say something, but he never did.

Finally I couldn't stand the tension anymore. "What do you want?" It came out meaner than I'd intended.

Luke pulled himself up to his full height, like he was readying himself for battle. Then he said, "Nobody puts Baby in the corner." His face was serious for a moment, but then he broke out into a huge grin.

I couldn't help it. I snorted in my milk.

"Did you just Patrick Swayze my daughter?" my dad asked, from the other side of the table.

Luke gave another cocky grin. "Sure did."

Chuckles began to erupt from my dad's body. His shoulders shook as he stood there laughing until I couldn't hear him laugh anymore. All I could hear was him wheezing. Dad's face was red, and his eyes were squinted shut as tears ran down his cheeks. He hit his hand on the table as if that would make it stop. The man was cracking up—literally.

It wasn't that funny, but Luke and I couldn't stop laughing either. Eventually we all pulled ourselves together.

"OK, OK," Luke finally said. "I came here for a reason."

Uh-oh, he's definitely going to yell at me now.

"I'm sorry!" I blurted. "I know I screwed it up. All that work we did together. You were so nice to me and helped me, and I just ran off. I threw it all away."

"Yeah, we need to work on that whole running away thing you do." He smiled. "It's weird . . . but that's not why I'm here."

"Then why are you here?"

Luke ignored me and turned to my dad. "Can Micah be excused from the table?"

Dad just shrugged. "If she wants to." He looked in my direction.

"What happened to the water hose?" I asked.

He smiled. "It's out of order."

CHAPTER 39

9 days left

It felt good to be out of the house. Luke didn't have his skateboard with him, so we set off on foot. I took in a deep breath as we walked, letting the warm breeze blow my hair all around me. The sun was setting, and everything was bathed in a warm orange glow, and for some reason it made me feel all fuzzy inside.

Out of the corner of my eye I caught Luke watching me. "Where are we going?" I asked as we passed his street. I had just assumed that we were going to his house.

"You'll see," he said, charging ahead.

I could feel the heat of the sun still radiating from the sidewalk, and I welcomed the mist that came off the sprinklers we passed along the way. We walked quietly together for a while, listening to the sounds of summer. Then, out of the blue, Luke looked over at me again and said, "Megan heard her, you know."

"Who?" I asked. "What are you talking about?"

"Trish . . . Megan heard what she said to you on the field the other day. During tryouts."

I looked down. *Oh.*

"Megan was so mad. I've never seen her that furious. She was about to go off on Trish, but another girl beat her to it."

I looked at Luke, confused.

"That Libby girl," he added. "The one who hangs out with Trish's new friends. She let them all have it."

"Really?" My voice sounded small. I couldn't believe it.

Luke nodded. "She started to chase after you too, but her mom held her back." He looked down for a moment. "I was going to follow you, but your dad said he wanted to talk to you alone."

I was in shock. I stopped paying attention to where we were going as I thought about what he'd said. Maybe my friendship with Libby wasn't as lost as I'd thought.

Suddenly Luke and I were turning a corner, and I realized where we were going: the pool.

"I don't have my bathing suit," I said, noticing for the first time that Luke was wearing his swim trunks.

He looked guiltily over at me. "Yeah . . . I forgot to tell you to bring one." He winced. "Sorry."

"Isn't the pool closed? It's late."

"Technically it should be, but today was the luau. It's an end-of-summer tradition." He grinned.

By the time we got to the gated entrance, the sun had nearly set. A few tired-looking families were still trickling out, and a little girl wearing a grass skirt and an itty-bitty coconut bra waddled past us.

I looked at Luke, and he laughed. "Told ya," he said. "We didn't want you to miss it just because you were too busy being a hermit crab."

I blushed.

As we passed through the entrance, I noticed that the lifeguard shack had been decorated with lanterns and fake flowers. Luke waved at Andre, who was behind the counter. "Thanks for waiting for us."

"No problem." Andre grinned. "We couldn't have a luau without the kahuna!"

When I saw the pool, I stopped and stared. The sunset had slowly shifted from oranges and pinks to purples and blues, and the pool looked completely different at night. The underwater lights were on, and the light reflecting out of the water made everything seem sparkly and special.

I looked over to my usual spot—more out of habit than anything else—and was surprised to see Megan and Ava waiting with the rest of the boys. They all looked excited to see me as Luke and I walked up.

"There she is!" Josh said, throwing his arms in the air. "We thought you were dead or something."

Megan scowled at him, then looked up at me and smiled. "Hey." She scooted closer to Ava and patted her towel for me to have a seat. I sat down, feeling almost as nervous as I had the first time they'd invited me to join them.

Ryan scooted over next to me and nudged me with his shoulder. "Glad you made it."

Luke sat across from me. "We were about to go for a night swim, but it just felt wrong without you here."

I looked down at the T-shirt and shorts I was wearing. "I don't have a swimsuit—" I started to say, but the boys were already grabbing me by my hands and feet. "Or a towel!" I finished as they carried me toward the pool and swung me from my hands and legs.

"That doesn't matter." Josh grunted under my weight. "Dang, Micah, how much do your feet weigh?"

The boys started counting as they swung me like a human hammock. "One! Two!"

"Wait!" I squealed.

I was drowned out by the splash of water as it rushed around me. When my head broke the surface, everyone was screaming and laughing. Then they all jumped in after me.

Charlie and Andre sat on the edge of the pool and let

their feet dangle in the water while they watched us swim. "You can use my towel," Charlie offered. "Just give it back to me at Tuesday's practice."

"Wait, what?" I asked, dodging Josh as he tried to dunk me.

Charlie smiled. "You didn't know? I'm the assistant coach for Xpress."

My heart leapt for joy. Then I felt it sink all over again. It would have been awesome having Charlie as a coach. Now I was going to miss out on that too.

"I didn't make the team," I said, letting my face sink into the water a bit.

"What do you mean?" Megan turned to face me. "Yes, you did!"

"No I didn't. I ran off, remember?"

Megan was staring at me now. "Didn't you look at the posting online? You made the cut, Micah!" she said, laughing at the look on my face.

I gripped the side of the pool. "But . . . how?"

Josh swam around like a shark. "You must have impressed them when you schooled that Marissa girl. I told you. You're a straight up *haus*."

"You're on the list," Charlie assured me. She pulled it up on her phone. "Your name is right here. McKinney, right?"

"Holy crap!" I lost my grip and sank under but popped my head back up and sputtered. "You're kidding me!"

Ryan laughed. "You really didn't know?"

"Is that why you were avoiding us?" Luke asked.

"I just told them you were PMSing or something," Josh said, floating on his back.

I ignored him. "Did everybody who tried out make the team?"

"Not everyone," Charlie said. "Coach Tremble was made aware of a situation at tryouts, and it forced him to make a few tough decisions. We have a zero-tolerance policy when it comes to bullying."

"Trish is off the team," Ava said. I could tell that she was trying to hide how sad she was about it.

"I'm sorry," I said.

"Don't be," Megan said, suddenly stern. "She deserves it after what she said to you." She shook her head. "She's changed. She didn't use to be like that."

Marissa has a way of doing that to people, I thought.

"That Marissa girl didn't make it either," Ava said, reading my mind. "But Samantha and Libby did."

I thought of Libby again, and wondered if what Luke had said about her standing up for me was true. Things could never go back to the way they were. But maybe that was OK. Maybe someday we could start to build something new.

"OK, guys, time is almost up," Andre said, looking at his watch. "You've got until ten o'clock, and then you have to get out."

We had been at the pool longer than I'd thought. My fingers were wrinkly, and the stars had come out. Luke swam toward me like an alligator. "One more chance," he said, lifting his face out of the water.

"One more chance for what?" I asked.

"For me to win back the kahuna title. Micah McKinney, I challenge you to a breath-holding contest."

I rolled my eyes.

"Just one more time." He grabbed my hands and pulled me through the water with him. "Please."

My stomach flipped. "OK, fine."

"Ready?" He breathed.

I nodded.

We both went under, still holding hands. I opened my eyes under the water, just like I had in the beginning of the summer, and once again I could see Luke looking right back at me. My T-shirt kept billowing in the water, causing me to float, but Luke pulled me down toward him, bringing his face dangerously close to mine. My heart about leaped out of my chest. Bubbles leaked out of Luke's mouth and tickled my face, causing me to come up for air giggling.

"I won!" he shouted.

"You cheated!" I shouted back, splashing him.

He swam at me and dunked me underwater. "I'm the kahuna!" he shouted.

"Sorry, buddy," Andre said. "Your time was up. It's ten-oh-three—pool's closed. You'll just have to try again another time."

"What?" Luke screamed.

Everybody laughed at him.

"Come on! Get out! We've got places to go," Andre said, looking at Charlie sitting next to him.

We all climbed out of the water and scrambled for our towels as we made our way toward the exit.

"Popsicles on the house," Andre said. "To celebrate the kahuna making the team."

We all rushed forward and raided the freezer in the lifeguard hut.

"Luke!" Megan suddenly shouted, looking at her phone. "You didn't tell Mom where we were? She's freaking out."

"Oops." Luke shrugged. "I guess I forgot."

"She's so mad! Look at this!" She held out her phone to show him the notifications.

"Crap, we'd better go." Luke went to Andre and said, "Thanks again, man."

Andre smiled. "No problem." He motioned toward me with a Popsicle. "Anything for the kahuna."

Luke winked at me, then turned toward Josh. "Come on, dude, we have to go!"

Josh turned around, holding a Popsicle in each hand. "Way to tick off your mom when my parents are out of town, and I have to spend the night."

"Shut up and get moving before she comes looking for us," Luke said.

"Too late," Megan said, pointing to the SUV sitting in the pool parking lot.

"Great," Luke mumbled.

We had all made our way out the gated exit when I realized I'd left my flip-flops sitting by the pool. I turned around to get them but stopped when I saw Andre standing in front of Charlie, kissing her. It was a real kiss—like the movie-star kind—with his hands on both sides of her face.

I turned away, embarrassed. I wasn't supposed to see that. There was no way I was walking past now. I'd rather go barefoot.

I walked out to the parking lot to see everyone piling into the SUV.

"Do you want a ride?" Sandi asked out her open window.

"That's OK," I said. "It's a nice night. I think I'd like to walk."

She looked like she wanted to insist, but Keaton was with her, and the car was full. "OK," she said doubtfully. "But be careful."

Ryan got out of the car. "I'll walk with her. It's on my way home anyway."

"I'll go too," Luke said, starting to crawl out.

Sandi's face transformed into that scary look moms get sometimes. "I don't think so, bub." Then she turned to me with a smile. "Bye, sweetie, be careful going home now."

* * *

Ryan and I slipped right back into our easy way. The stars were even brighter now. As we walked, I kept thinking about that kiss I'd accidentally seen between Charlie and Andre. Would you feel different after a kiss like that? Like you were carrying it around with you everywhere you went? Then I started thinking about Luke pulling me through the water until his face was right up to mine, wondering if he had done it on purpose . . . wishing he had.

"What are you thinking about?" Ryan asked out of nowhere.

I jerked my Popsicle away from my mouth. "Nothing."

My cheeks burned in the dark, and I glanced over at him, hoping he believed me.

We eventually fell back into stride, and I felt myself relax again. Then Ryan broke the silence. "I know you like Luke."

"What?" I started. "No, I don't."

He laughed. "Yeah, you do."

I felt myself blush again.

"You get this dreamy look on your face every time you're around him."

"No, I don't!"

"It's OK," Ryan said, but he looked a little sad. "I think he likes you too."

I didn't know what to say, so I didn't say anything at all. I had always been comfortable around Ryan, and I didn't want to ruin anything by talking. Instead, I enjoyed the taste of my cherry Popsicle and the sounds of summer as we made our way home, all the while wondering if what he'd said was true.

CHAPTER 40

I day left

I looked at my calendar and couldn't believe it was almost here. Tomorrow was the day I'd been waiting for. I'd wake up and magically be thirteen, and ready or not, I'd be walking through the doors of a brand-new school.

To commemorate the occasion, Dad gave me my own phone as an early birthday gift. He promised me we'd have my party the next weekend, after the first-day-of-school rush was over.

I was sitting on my bed, looking for free meditation apps, when Megan called and invited me over. She and Ava wanted to pick out what we were all going to wear the next day. I'd already picked my outfit out that morning: plain white shirt, a pair of flattering shorts that showed off my strong legs, and my mom's red high tops. How could I not? They were my lucky shoes.

"Micah, come on!" Megan pleaded. "We can't pick out outfits without you."

I snorted. "Oh yeah, because I have such great fashion sense?"

"Just get your butt over here."

I giggled. "OK, I'll be there in a minute."

I walked out to the living room, where my dad was watching TV. "What are you up to, kiddo?" he asked. "Wanna have a movie night before your big day?"

"Actually, Megan just called. She wants me to come over to pick out first-day-of-school outfits."

"That sounds awful."

"Tell me about it," I pretended to grumble. "So, can I go?"

"It's fine by me. Just don't stay out too late."

"I won't," I said.

I stepped out of the front door and started to grab my longboard from the porch but changed my mind. I made my way to the garage instead and pulled out my trusty old bike. I decided right then and there that I was definitely going to ride it to school the next day. Who cared what anyone else had to say? I was never going to be too old to ride it.

As I rode to Megan's house, I thought about how different the neighborhood looked now that I was used to it. It had felt so weird when I'd first moved in. But now, among the familiar sounds of late summer, it felt like home. The humid air rushed past my ears as I peddled faster and faster. I felt weightless, without a care in the world.

I pulled into Megan's driveway and swerved just in time to avoid Keaton's Rollerblades. Luke was sitting out front.

"Hey, dork," he said, standing up to meet me. "Nice ride."

"Hey." I couldn't help the smile that sprouted on my face. I kicked my rusty kickstand about twenty times until it finally gave.

Luke held out his hand to me. "Come with me real quick."

"Where are we going?" I asked, taking his hand and completely forgetting why I'd come to his house in the first place.

"You'll see," he said, linking his fingers through mine and leading me to the backyard.

Luke led me passed his mother's garden toward a wooded area in the corner of the yard that flickered with the last lightning bugs that remained from summer. Hidden among the bushes was a bench that I had never seen, even though I had spent nearly every day of summer training in this backyard.

"This was my secret hideout when I was little," he said,

winking at me. "You should be honored that I'm sharing it with you."

I smiled.

"I got you something." Luke let go of my hand and sat down on the bench, gesturing for me to take a seat. We were shrouded in the privacy of our own little forest in the corner of the yard.

"What is it?" I asked, watching him reach under the bench.

"Well, actually I have two things. The first is this . . ." He pulled out two homemade Funfetti cupcakes and handed one to me. "Happy birthday," he said.

I blushed. "My birthday is tomorrow."

"I know." He grinned. "I just wanted to be the first one to say it."

We sat there together, leaning back on the bench, enjoying our cupcakes. We were so close that I could feel the heat of Luke's leg through his jeans as it leaned against mine.

I couldn't help but grin at him as I picked off sprinkles and ate them one by one. "So what's the other thing?"

"Geez. Greedy much?" Luke laughed but reached under the bench anyway to get whatever he had hidden there. "OK, close your eyes."

"Why?"

"Just do it," he said, being bossy as usual.

I did as I was told and felt him getting closer. I could

swear his face was right in front of mine, because I could smell his shampoo. It made me think of that moment in the pool.

Is he about to kiss me? I tried to open one eye to see how far away from me he was.

"Nuh-uh-uh-uh," Luke said. "Keep 'em closed."

"What are you doing?" I asked. The suspense was killing me. I didn't like having my eyes closed while his were open.

"You'll see. . . . OK, now open them."

When I opened my eyes, Luke was sitting in front of me holding two lit sparklers. I laughed out loud.

"You missed the fireworks this year, so I thought . . . I don't know." He suddenly sounded nervous.

"I love it!" I reached for one of the sparklers, and together we twirled them in the air, writing our names into the growing dark. Mine fizzled out first, and I could have sworn Luke was in the middle of writing my name when his died out too.

We sat there facing each other for a minute. I wasn't sure, but I thought maybe Luke was leaning closer to me. I must have been leaning toward him too, because I could smell the vanilla on his breath.

He grinned. "I have a secret to tell you."

"What?"

"I lied. I've actually never kissed a girl before."

I couldn't help the smile that was spreading across my face.

"I know we just met this summer, but I think you're my best friend, Micah." He suddenly sounded serious.

"I think you're my best friend too," I whispered.

Luke looked down at the burned-out sparkler in his hand. It seemed like there was something more that he wanted to say, so I just waited.

Finally he looked up at me, and his eyes were greener than ever. "There's something I feel like I need to do, but I shouldn't."

"What?"

"You know Ryan is my other best friend, right?"

"Yeah?"

"He really likes you."

Now it was my turn to look down at the burned-out sparkler. I didn't like the idea of hurting Ryan.

"But I like you too," Luke continued. "I always have."

I looked up at him. Gone was the cocky boy who winked at girls. In his place sat a boy with pleading eyes.

Luke put the sparkler stick down on the bench and leaned forward so that his elbows rested on his knees. He put his head between his hands and ran his fingers through his hair. He stayed that way for a minute. Then he sat up and looked straight ahead. It almost seemed as if he were talking to himself when he said, "I want you to be my friend,

Micah, and I want Ryan to be my friend." He sighed. "But I really want to kiss you. If I do that, maybe I won't want to kiss you all the time like I do now. Maybe then I'll be over it, and Ryan won't be mad at me. And then maybe we can all go back to hanging out like nothing happened."

I didn't say anything. I didn't want him to be over it, but I also didn't want to hurt Ryan's feelings.

Luke looked over at me, and I could see that he was nervous. "Aren't you going to say anything?" he asked.

I didn't know what to say. I could feel myself leaning closer to him until our noses were barely touching, and then I quickly kissed him on the lips. It lasted a nanosecond and felt like the brush of a feather. Our eyes were still open, watching each other. I watched his mouth as it transformed into a slow, lazy grin.

"Don't tell anyone," I whispered.

Luke smiled bigger and placed both of his hands on either side of my face, just like Andre had done to Charlie, and kissed me longer. This time I closed my eyes. I thought my heart was going to explode. Luke's lips were cool and soft, and when he pulled away, vanilla lingered on my lips too. We both just sat there for a minute.

"We won't tell anyone," he said, a little breathless. Then he looked at me and grinned bigger than ever. "We'd better go. Everyone's waiting for you."

"What do you mean?"

"Let's just say I'm not the one who made cupcakes for you." He gave his devilish grin with the slight eyebrow wiggle. "I'll go through the back, and you can go through the front. If they ask what took you so long, just say you were out riding your rickety old bike."

Luke winked at me and ran toward the back door. I just sat there for a minute. I couldn't believe what had just happened. I waited for a moment and checked to see if the kiss was still there. It was. I wondered how long it would last.

CHAPTER 41

I day left

I didn't bother ringing the doorbell or knocking on the front door. When I walked into the Waters's living room, I was surprised to see my dad standing there, along with the rest of my friends and the Waters family.

"SURPRISE!" everyone shouted.

Sandi walked toward me, holding a cupcake with a lit candle on top. As she approached, Luke quickly rubbed his thumb across my chin to swipe a bit of icing off it.

"You've got a little something on your chin." He grinned.

Ryan looked from Luke to me and then back to Luke. Luke noticed and promptly punched me in the shoulder. "Just kidding," he said.

"Ow!"

"Luke, don't punch the birthday girl!" Sandi scolded.

After cake, I got to open the presents everyone had gotten me. Makeup and sunglasses from Ava, a phone case from the Waters family, and a cup and jockstrap from Josh, who laughed so hard when I opened it and asked, "What *is* this?!"

"You can't be the big kahuna without one of these, right?" he asked, cracking himself up.

I didn't even notice that I hadn't opened a gift from Ryan until my dad and I were headed out the door to leave. Dad was outside loading my bike into the back of the truck when Ryan caught up to me.

"Hey, Micah," he said. "Happy birthday." He handed me a package but wouldn't look me in the eye.

"Thanks," I said, slowly taking it from him. The way he handed it to me made it seem like something special.

Ryan lingered for a bit, like he had something he wanted to say. Finally he shoved his hands in his pockets and mumbled, "See you tomorrow."

"OK." I smiled at him. "See ya."

I started to leave but surprised myself by turning around and giving him a quick hug. When I got into Dad's truck, I saw Ryan still standing there, watching us drive off.

I didn't open his gift right away when I got home. For some reason, it made me nervous. Instead, I washed my face and brushed my teeth. I waited until I was snuggled into my bed before opening his gift. It was a leather journal with a magnolia blossom carved into the cover. I opened the cover to find a drawing on the first page. It was me, lying in the grass in the shade of my magnolia tree with my eyes closed, smiling a little bit to myself. It was just the way the boys had found me on that first day of summer . . . minus the drool and grass, of course.

I looked beautiful.

I turned off my lamp and leaned back on my pillow, thinking of that long-ago day. The warm breeze from my open window brought with it the lemonlike scent of the magnolia tree, even though the blossoms had faded long ago.

* * *

This is how it's going to happen. I'm going to walk into seventh grade with my new friends from my new neighborhood, and I'll be a completely different girl.

Eighty-two days will have passed—just the time I needed to figure myself out. Just enough time to realize that it doesn't matter what happened last year or the year before that. It won't matter what I'm wearing or whether I have boobs. None of it will matter because I'll be too excited looking forward to what comes next.

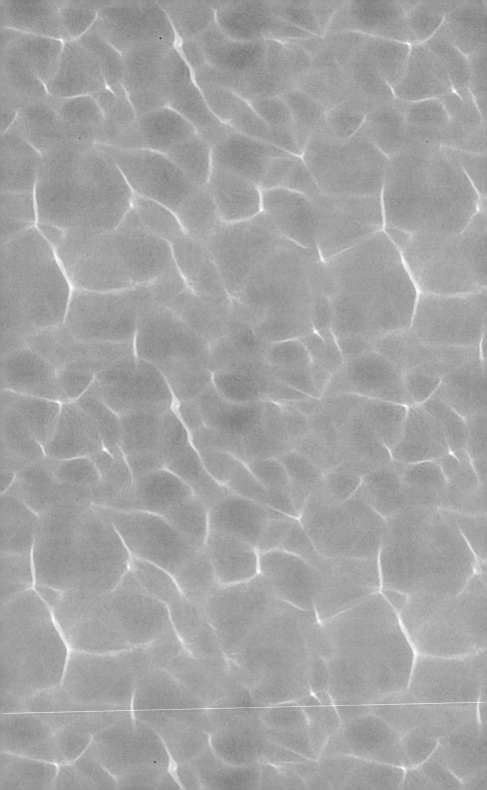

Acknowledgments

This book started out as a sample "slice of life" assignment for my language arts students and was simply about a girl at the pool with a wedgie and a crush. If it had not been for my students urging me to answer the question, "What happens next?" I never would have had the courage to turn this into a book. To my students, past and present, thank you. Thank you for teaching me as much as I've taught you and for inspiring me to be the best version of myself I can possibly be. When I look at the world through your eyes, all I see are never-ending posibilites.

To my daughters: Bridget, you were Micah's first best friend, and I've loved watching the two of you grow together over the years. You are the ultimate authority, and your opinion on how this book turns out matters to me the most. I can't wait to see the stories in your head come to fruition too. Little Miss Penelope, I don't want you to grow up any more than you already have, but I can't wait for you to meet Micah too. With your spunk and adventurous spirit, I have a feeling the two of you will get along just fine. Being your mother has made me a better person.

I'm forever grateful to my agent, Elizabeth Bennett, who gifted me her time and patience in order to teach me how to polish this rough gem into a book. Thank you to Jill Corcoran, who saw promise in Micah's voice and brought Elizabeth and me together. You both have given me more than you will ever know.

To Alison Deering, I could not have asked for a better editor. You helped me dig deep and feel emotions I've refused to feel for years. I never intended this story to be about a girl dealing with the aftermath of her mother's death, because that was my reality, one I'd spent my whole life hiding from. Telling Micah's story, in a way, was an avenue for telling my own, a painful yet cathartic experience that was long overdue.

Thank you to designer Hilary Wacholz and cover artist Mirelle Ortega, who helped bring the image of Micah McKinney to life. I cried happy tears when I saw her face for the first time. I also couldn't have come this far without my critique partners, Suzanne Nieman Brown and Rebecca Marks Rudy. Your insights have been invaluable.

Emily Gipson, my partner in dreaming, may we continue to swing in the park, hike in the mountains (preferably sans rattlesnakes), and share our dreams with one another until we're good and old. You have taught me what it means to turn a dream into a goal and that goal into a plan. I always knew you would do great things. What I didn't expect was for you to inspire me to do great things too.

This book is ultimately about family and friendship and how those relationships help to shape a person. I wouldn't be the person I am today without the love and support of the following people: my dad, Walter Gwyn, whose love has no bounds, and Alyson Gwyn, sister and partner in crime. All I see is laughter and love when I think of growing up with you.

To the Chapmans, who took me in and loved me fiercely. You are seriously the best in-laws in all the land. Thank you for being early readers and encouraging me with all your hearts. With you by my side, life will always be an adventure full of rooftop rescues, impromptu Rollerblading sessions, and dam swims.

Unlike Micah, I have never been wanting for friends, having been blessed at a young age with true friendship— the kind that embraces you at your worst and celebrates you at your best. Sarah (Trotter) Stewart, Mickey Matlock, Amy (Burket) Wolfe, Tara (Land) Wood, Brandi (Farquar) Gjoni, and Brooke Gray—growing up with you gave me some of the best years of my life. The person I have become is due, in part, to you and our youthful adventures.

Andrea Skinner, Kari Johnson, Amanda Scalbom, Kim Bolton, Gail Barron, Sandi Rhynard—you are the most uplifting women I know. You give so much of yourselves in your efforts to uplift other people, and I'm not ashamed to say I have been the recipient of your selfless love and support.

And finally, to the love of my life, Brent Chapman. You swept me away and led me to a life I never knew I could have. I can't wait to see what kind of surprises life has in store for us as we continue our adventure together. Your love and support mean the world to me.

About the Author

Nina Chapman spends most of her days teaching middle school, where she has discovered a talent for thriving in the awkward. When she's not gathering feedback from her student test audience, she's reading books or playing outside. Her favorite activities include hot-air balloon gazing, barefoot bike riding, and getting lost in the woods. Nina took the scenic route to teaching, first obtaining a bachelor's degree in creative writing from the University of Colorado Denver. A member of Rocky Mountain Chapter of the Society of Children's Book Writers and Illustrators, she currently lives in the Denver, Colorado, area with her husband, two daughters, and a pitbull pound puppy.